Mission: Find Mum

Happy reading!

Jo Somerset

Jo Somerset

Stairwell Books //

Published by Stairwell Books
161 Lowther Street
York, YO31 7LZ

www.stairwellbooks.co.uk
@stairwellbooks

Cover art and illustrations: Dawn Treacher

ISBN: 978-1-913432-94-2
p6

Advanced Reader Copy

To young seekers everywhere.

CHAPTER 1

NOTE

Isla burst through the front door and flung her bag on the bottom stair.

"Mum!" she yelled. "I told Ally to go stuff herself!"

She kicked the door shut.

"Mum! I did it! Just like we talked about. I'm not gonna let her get to me anymore."

No answer. She slipped off her shoes.

Oh yeah, Tuesday. Mum was on late shift.

Isla yanked her tie over her head and jogged through the living room to the kitchen. Nice, Mum had done the washing up. She took a glass from the drainer, poured juice from the fridge and glugged it down. It was boiling hot outside. Through the window, the sunflowers in the back garden nodded, gasping for water.

She breathed in the cool silence of the house. She sniffed and smiled as a trace of yesterday's macaroni cheese hung in the air. Just ten days until the end of Year 7. She rinsed the glass and as it clattered on the draining board, she remembered: nine days until the school concert. A feeling of unease fizzed in her throat at the thought of standing alone on stage playing her trumpet.

Better do some practice before Lac gets home and starts wailing at the noise. Isla clumped upstairs to her room. Who'd want a little brother? On the landing, panic jolted through her – her bedroom door was open. Weasley could have escaped. She darted into her room and – phew! There he was, snuffling around the hamster wheel, bits of hay stuck on his ginger fur. Last Christmas he'd been missing for two nightmare days behind the skirting board. She poked her finger through the bars of the cage.

'Hey little buddy, I'm gonna make a big noise now, so you can go in Lac's room.' Since she got her hamster last birthday, she told him everything. He was named after Ron Weasley because of his red hair. As she turned, cage in her arms, something caught her eye. It was a note on her pillow.

'Gone away for a few days. I've arranged for you to stay at Aunty Lou's. Sorry.'

Mum's handwriting. Isla put the cage on the floor. Her heart did a double thump. She held the note between two fingers as if it might self-destruct and swept her long hair back with the other hand.

Sometimes Mum left notes on her bed. Things like 'Don't forget swimming things', 'Change Weasley's bedding' or 'Hoover your room'. Occasionally she left 'Love yoooo', with hearts and kisses, which Isla saved in her golden box in the wardrobe. But she'd never left a note like this.

Isla read the note over and over. Why hadn't Mum texted? She held the note to her nose, smelt it, and laid it down carefully. Something wasn't right. Then it dawned on her. Mum didn't say where she'd gone.

She punched in Mum's number on her phone. No ring tone, just a flat voice:

'We are unable to connect you.'

Isla slid down the wall and sat with her legs stretched out in front of her. She couldn't even leave a message. What now? Mum never ran out of battery and always rang back if Isla called her. She opened the cage and scooped the hamster into her cupped hands.

What would Aunty Lou say? She wasn't a real aunty, just Mum's friend and Lac's after-school childminder. They'd never stayed at hers before. Isla pictured sleeping in Lou's grown-up sons' old bedroom, sharing with Lac and all his toys. How would she do her trumpet practice, let alone homework? And what about Weasley? None of this made sense. She called again. No answer.

The doorbell's ring pierced her ear, and she winced as it made her hearing aid whine. Downstairs, Weasley snuffling around her collar, she opened the door to Aunty Lou's husband, Dave, and Lac. Her little brother pushed past her.

'Oi, shoes off!' she yelled.

He ducked under the coats hanging in the hall and disappeared into the front room. Before any vrooms and gunfire started up, Isla knew he was on his latest game.

'I know you're supposed to be staying with us, but will you tell your mum that the hospital just called. Lou has to go for her operation tomorrow so we can't have you until after the holidays. Lou's messaged your mum but can you remind her as well.'

Isla was still stunned by Mum's note. She couldn't think of anything to say except, 'Okay. Bye.'

She closed the door and rested her forehead in the space where Mum's coat should be. High-pitched shouts and grunts flowed from the living room as Lac fought off his enemies, one by one.

Isla called Mum again, holding the phone to each ear in turn, as if that would make a difference. It didn't.

CHAPTER 2

MISSING

'Where's Mum?' Lac asked, eyes fixed to the screen.

'Doing an extra shift at the hospital. I've got to get your tea and put you to bed. She'll be back later.'

Lac slammed his controller on the floor. 'I don't want your smelly scran. I want Mum's.'

'It's all the same food. Come on, our kid, you know Mum has to work.' Isla gritted her teeth. She was fed up with trying to keep Lac calm. Now she had to cover for Mum as well – again. *Why me?*

Lac stared at the screen.

'Tell you what, let's look in the freezer, and you choose a pizza.'

Lac slid the zip of his Aston Villa hoody up and down, while the frozen images on the television hung mid-battle. Isla stood behind the settee and felt an urge to lay the hamster in her brother's mop of curly hair. It looked like an ideal nest, and she giggled at the thought that Weasley might get lost, being the same ginger colour as Lac's hair.

'And you can put it in the microwave,' she added. 'We won't tell Mum.'

Her brother slithered onto his knees, chucked the controller in its box, and took Isla's hand as he stood up.

'I'll tell Mum tonight that you've been dead good,' she said.

Isla didn't know why she lied. Even though the note said 'a few days,' she hoped Mum would come home that night.

There wasn't an adult she could ask for help. Nana was too busy looking after poorly Grandpa. As for phoning Aunty Lou, well, she was the problem in the first place. If she wasn't going for an operation, she'd be minding them right now. It must be serious – she'd never let them down before.

Lac brushed his teeth and grumbled when he got into bed.

'Where's Mum?'

'Told you. At work.'

He turned on his side to face the wall, and said to Luke Skywalker on his pillow, 'She better come and say goodnight when she's back.'

'She will.' Isla swallowed, glad that Lac couldn't see her face. She had no idea what state Mum would be in when she returned. If she came back.

Isla sat on her floor, her eyes locked with Weasley's inside his cage.

'I can't tell anyone. They'll think it really weird that Mum's just left a note to say she was going away, and awful that her phone is switched off,' she told him. Isla unlocked the cage and cradled the hamster in the crook of her arm like a tiny baby. Most days Mum was just like any other mum, reminding Isla about Scouts or trumpet lesson, calling her 'Babs' even though Isla hated that babyish name. Even Lac wasn't a babby anymore.

She nestled her nose in Weasley's fur. Mum did sometimes go off into her own world. Not speaking. Going out without telling them when she'd be back. It wasn't weird, it was just Mum. Even during Mum's 'down' days, when she lay on her bed with the door closed, they knew she was still there and would come out in the end.

But Mum had never gone off and not come back. An image flashed into Isla's head of a poster she passed every day on the way to school. A set of photos, and underneath each one a name, date and the message: *Have you seen her (or him)?* Some had been missing for months. A wormy feeling crawled around in Isla's stomach. The wriggling sensation suddenly intensified, and she nearly puked.

She dumped Weasley in his cage and leapt to her wardrobe. She pulled her golden box from its hiding place. Under the notes from Mum, attendance certificates and her bag of baby teeth, she uncovered a smaller cardboard box. The tape holding it closed was still in place. Phew! Mum hadn't found it and gone off in a huff.

Weasley scuffling in his hay made her think of Mum. Usually she was on the move, just like him. Sitting on the bed, she closed her eyes and pictured Mum nodding her head in time to music on the radio. Mum herding them to the front door in their school uniforms, Mum taking her to the hearing clinic, Mum stirring a pan on the cooker, Mum swearing when Lac broke a toy. Mum brushing her hair, Mum talking on the phone, Mum bending to kiss her goodnight.

Isla opened her eyes again. She didn't want to picture Mum being still as a statue, staring at the wall and not saying goodnight when Isla went upstairs to bed. Her lips would set in a tight frozen line if Isla mentioned Dad, so she'd given up asking about him.

She could still remember his gravelly voice and the scrape of stubble from his chin against her face. Her first memory was flying: Dad throwing her in the air and catching her. The clouds above and Dad's huge hands holding strong around her middle, shouting,

"Who's my bonnie girl?"

Isla clutched the box on her knee. Up in the air, screaming, Dad's hands catching her, hiccups taking over. She always got hiccups when she was scared. Deep down, some part of her didn't believe he was dead. She imagined him far away in another country. Still there somewhere, even though she knew he wasn't.

She peeled back the tape on the smaller box, opened the lid and unfolded the top letter that she wrote last week.

'Dear Dad,

Drama was brilliant today. Miss Henry said me and Kayla were like pros with our comedy act. You know my new zinger? It's brilliant, I can hear almost everything. I won't need to sit at the front of class next term, which means no more 'Oddball!' heckles from Ally next to me. Hurray! It's nearly school holidays and I'm going to my SECOND Scout Camp in August. Remember the first camp last Easter, when I FROZE?

Lac's still mad for Star Wars. He got a Luke Skywalker and a full-size lightsaber for his birthday. I actually managed to play 'Happy Birthday' to him on my trumpet.

Mum is alright most of the time. She never says, but I think she misses you.

Wish you were here.

Lots of love,

Isla xxxxx'

Isla re-folded the letter, laid it back on top of the others and smoothed the sticky tape back in place. She'd never told anyone about the letters. She knew people would think she was crazy writing to someone who was dead, but she didn't care. Pretending he was alive made her feel like she still had a dad, like he didn't disappear when she was five.

Late that night, Isla sneaked into Mum's room and went through all her things, looking for clues. While rifling through a drawer of receipts and bills, Isla thought she might find her birth certificate. Mum had said it was lost when school asked for it at the start of Year Seven. But it wasn't there. No letters, either, that might show where Mum had gone. She gave up, opened the wardrobe and tried on Mum's green dress. Adding a splash of red lipstick, she smiled at her reflection in the dressing table mirror, but her hair was a mess. She and Mum had the same long hair, but Mum's was straighter and blacker. She reached her arm out but the hairbrush was gone.

Mum's jewellery box sat on a shelf. Isla lifted the lid and pulled out the top section. A chunky silver ring that she had never seen before lay at the bottom. Isla traced the ring's long cross, surrounded by a patterned circle with her fingertip. It hung loosely on her middle finger. She put Mum's nightie and the ring under her pillow and cried until she fell asleep.

CHAPTER 3

FIGHT

Next morning, in between stuffing his mouth with Cheerios, Lac asked twenty times,

'Where's Mum?'

Each time Isla replied, 'Away.'

She wanted to say, 'I don't know.'

Isla was scared that if she told any adults, they'd take her and Lac away, and Mum wouldn't know where they were. Mum might need help. What sort of help, she didn't know. It wasn't the usual help, ringing in sick and taking Lac to school, then sorting the shopping and cooking while Mum slept all day. She wished she could tell Kayla. As besties they always helped each other sort things out, but it was too risky.

She dropped Lac off at his school gate and dashed for the bus, but she still had to sneak in halfway through a lesson. Miss Henry pretended not to notice. Isla was half-relieved when she saw Kayla's seat was empty. She laid her phone on her knee under the desk and tapped.

wassup? u ok?

Got bad tum. u?

Ok. Got next Harry Potter. Order of the Phoenix.

I want it after u

K. miss u at skul.

miss u too. Tell u wot.

wot?

I don't miss Ally's lot

they miss u lol😂🙌

haha shame

c u soon?😁😝👆

Ye few days lol

'...not too early to start thinking about what you want to do when you leave school. Isla, what about you?'

'Uh.' Isla lifted her head. 'I want to be a musician, Miss.' She had wanted to be a poet after she won a poetry prize in Year 6, but last autumn she saw a trumpet player who was deaf in a visiting band. Since then, her dream was to join the National Youth Jazz Orchestra.

'Really? That's quite an ambition.' Before Miss Henry could say anything else, the bell rang for break.

Outside, Ally and her gang surrounded Isla.

'A musician!' Ally's spit spattered Isla's sleeve. 'They won't want a reject like you.' She pointed to Isla's zinger and stuck her finger in her ear as if she also had a hearing aid. 'You don't know nothing, Oddball!' she sneered, her face contorted like Draco Malfoy.

Oh no, I thought I'd sorted Ally. Isla's fingers clenched around the school's trumpet case.

'Oddball, Oddball,' the others said, fingers poking in their right ear.

Kayla, I need you.

'Go home and cry to mummy,' she jeered. 'Why don't you write a *poem* about howwible Ally?'

'Mummee, mummee! Ally's been howwible!' echoed in her ears.

Isla leant backwards……and swung the hard case with as much force as she could, catching Ally on her shoulder. At last, she was giving her enemy what she deserved. Ally staggered, fury flooding her face. She leapt forward, her long arms reaching for Isla's hair, with a scream that drilled through her zinger ear.

'FIGHT! FIGHT! FIGHT!' yelled a crowd of students who'd formed a circle around them.

Ally pushed Isla with both hands, and she fell backwards on top of the trumpet case with a loud 'CRACK!'. Picking herself up, she head-butted Ally in the stomach and tumbled onto the tarmac on top of her. Ally, spitting, squeezed her hands round Isla's throat. Isla's eyes rolled and felt her head go swimmy, then everything went into slow motion. Her eyes focused on soft flesh bulging from her opponent's sleeves. Isla bared her teeth, but before she could take a lump of flesh out of this revolting creature, the neck of her shirt choked her. Someone was yanking her up into a standing position.

'Inside! Straight to the Head's office.' It was the first time Isla had ever heard Miss Henry shout. Isla and Ally either side of her, she marched them across the playground and over the basketball court, to cries of 'What's happening, Miss?' from a group of lanky players who had stopped to watch.

The Head came straight to the point. Three-day exclusion. 'I'm phoning your parents to pick you up now.'

Isla felt it like another kick in the stomach. 'Umm, my Mum's at work, you can't get hold of her, Mrs Karim.'

'Right, you're in isolation until end of school. I'll call your mother this evening. Allison, wait outside my office until your carer comes for you.'

Isla sat in the isolation unit pretending to do her French homework. She was thinking about that word 'carer'. She remembered another conversation she'd had with Mum about Ally a few months back. That was when they had to sit together at the front of the class, so Isla could hear what was going on, and the teacher could keep an eye on Ally.

One day Ally had whispered, 'Your brother's name is pants.'

Isla said to Mum, 'I don't get it. What has Lac's name got to do with her?'

Mum explained, 'LAC stands for Looked After Children. Ally's a looked after child. Like several kids at your school.'

'Doesn't make sense, we're all looked after,' Isla had said.

'Ally lives with foster parents, not her real mum or dad, so she's Looked After with a capital L,' Mum said. Isla blinked. As she only had one parent, sometimes she felt an urge to hold on to Mum. But if you had NONE? She felt a bit sick.

'That's why you should be nice to Ally,' Mum said.

'No way,' Isla said, cuddling Weasley. But she kept thinking about it afterwards. Now she knew why Ally always talked about her 'fake parents' in a scathing voice.

The bell rang, and Isla remembered she had to pick up Lac from school. Head down, she pushed two fingers down her throat.

'Sir, I'm going to be sick,' she yelled, grabbed her bag and ran from the room. She barged through the crowds of students changing lessons, across the playground and out of the gate, arriving at the bus stop, bent over and coughing.

Back home, she and Lac watched David Attenborough's *Life of Birds*. Seeing birds sing to each other made her think about playing the trumpet. She didn't just enjoy the music; her trumpet notes sang out things she couldn't put into words.

On the next programme, Greta Thunberg talked about why she started school strikes to save the planet. Alongside Hermione Granger, who wasn't real, Greta was Isla's real-life hero. She said there was no Planet B, which sounded really random but made total sense when you thought about it.

CHAPTER 4

JUST ABOUT MANAGING

The landline was ringing but Isla didn't dare answer it. No way could she pretend to be Mum. For tea, she put cereal bowls on the table. They'd run out of Cheerios and had to make do with Weetabix, but Lac wouldn't eat it. He just said,

'When's she coming back?' over and over, until Isla screamed,

'I don't know, right? I don't know a thing. She's just gone.' She put her hand over her stupid gob.

His mouth opened and closed several times, like a bird's beak, except no sound came out. He ran upstairs and slammed his bedroom door. He emptied out his toybox onto the floor with a crash and yelled as he kicked each toy at the wall.

Isla's worst nightmare had come true. No parents. Like Ally.

Now what do I do, Mum?

Isla took the dishes to the kitchen. Her hands shook as she opened Weasley's cage, filled his food bowl and changed his water. She stood at the bottom of the stairs, her fists balled up, fingernails digging into her palms. *Don't cry*, she told herself, *we've got to keep going*. Hermione Granger would do something; she'd sort it out.

Up the stairs and into Lac's room, stepping over the mess of Hot Wheels and zombies and scattered Lego bricks, Isla sat on the bed. He sat beside her, holding Luke Skywalker in his fist. Isla covered his hand with hers, and he leant into her shoulder. They cried until their eyes were sore and their throats burned.

Isla made peanut butter toasties and took them back upstairs with an ice pop each, the luscious icy liquid cooling their raw throats. She climbed into Lac's bed and read Vulgar the Viking to him – the whole book. They snuggled up, like penguins in the David Attenborough film. Forgetting to take out her zinger, she drifted off, thinking Hermione would reckon she'd done okay.

A phone was ringing. Isla opened her eyes to unfamiliar diamond patterns made by the streetlight shining through Lac's curtains. Her body stiffened. She slid out of bed and followed the sound, but it wasn't her phone, it was the landline downstairs. It might be Mum. She picked up the handset.

'Mrs MacLean? I'm sorry to call so late, it's Mrs Karim here.'

Isla's sweaty fingers covered the mouthpiece. 'Mmmmfffmmm?' she said.

'Mrs MacLean?'

Isla grabbed a plastic bag and rustled it against the phone.

'I'm sorry, I can't hear you properly. I'll call you on your mobile first thing in the morning.'

She imagined the Head mouthing each word separately so Mum could hear.

Isla pressed the red cut-off button, then unplugged the phone's base-set from the wall. She sank onto the computer chair and wondered how long it would be before two strangers knocked on the door and took her and Lac away. Her fingers stroked the keyboard, rousing the machine from its sleep mode. She googled:

Where is Mum?

690 million results came up, all about a TV show called *Mum*.

She switched on the lights and rooted round the house for clues. A holdall bag was missing, but there were no letters in a pile of papers on the table or notes in Mum's work bag by her chair. Isla sat on the stairs, elbows on knees, facing the front door where Mum must have walked out.

Hermione would work it out. Hermione is smart, she'd learn a mum-returning spell under the old light in the school library, and be brave enough to utter the words, flick her wand and face a searing flash of light – but Hermione wasn't real. A living person had to find Mum. Anyway, nobody went to libraries anymore, everyone used –

Isla sat up straight. 'The computer!'

She ran into the living room and woke it up again. It took ages to look through the folders, and there was a lot she didn't understand. Nothing about a journey, and hardly anything in the last week. Isla tapped her fingers on the desk. She sat back and ran her fingers through her hair.

She leant forward again to give it one more try.

'Yessss.' The chair creaked as she bounced up and down. 'I've found some tickets. Emails in the recycle bin.'

Lac appeared at the door, barefoot, rubbing his eyes. 'Where is she?'

Isla peered at the screen and read out slowly: 'O-ban.'

'Where's that?' Lac leaned on her, looking at the screen.

'No wait, there's another email.'

Booking confirmation, CalMac Ferries. 'What the –?' Oban to Mora.

'What's ferries?'

'Like, ships sailing over the sea.' Over the sea? Isla googled Mora, and there it was, in the middle of a load of blue. The sea. Isla typed in 'Get directions – Oban to Mora'. A thick blue line curved up the coast and swept out to sea. And landed at a green blob – an island.

'Look,' Isla whispered. 'I think Mum's there.'

CHAPTER 5

FOR EMERGENCIES ONLY

Isla's eyes were drooping but she couldn't go back to bed. Lac slumped on the settee and reached for his iPad, muttering under his breath at each thrust and dodge, making explosion noises as he blasted his opponents.

Copying what Mum had done, Isla clicked 'Buy tickets' and fetched the secret credit card that Mum had shown her when she started high school.

'For an emergency,' Mum had said, in the same voice she'd used when showing her the stash of sanitary pads when she was in Year Six. 'Better to know. Just in case.'

Isla had felt queasy and hollow inside. Why did she need to know about the credit card?

'Probably won't need it.' Mum gave her a little hug, but Isla could tell her mind was elsewhere.

'Mum,' Isla had said, 'are you okay?'

Well, this *was* a flipping emergency, wasn't it? The passcode wasn't hard to remember as it was Isla's birthday. She clicked 'Download tickets' and entered her phone number.

Lac had keeled over on the settee, and she helped him climb the stairs then got back into bed with him.

Isla's eyes pinged open as daylight poured into the room. Her voice was still hoarse from all that crying, and she rang in sick from her mobile, the same as she'd done before when Mum was poorly. She made more peanut butter sarnies and took them back upstairs with two cans of Vimto. Mum wouldn't like them having pop for breakfast, but they had more important things to think about. Hermione would definitely be working out what to do next.

She put on a cheerful voice despite the sense of dread that had invaded her.

'Let's not wait any more for Mum to come back, let's go and find her. I've got tickets to where she is.'

Lac looked at her with big eyes. He jumped out of bed, tripped on some Lego, hopped back onto the bed and bounced up and down.

'We're going to find our Mum, find our Mum, find our Mum,' he sang, waving Luke Skywalker in the air.

They threw on jeans and t-shirts. Isla stretched her arms up high to pull the ladder from the loft and announced, 'I'm gonna find camping gear.' She couldn't keep the excitement out of her voice. This was really going to happen. Today. Isla was making it happen.

Lac held the ladder while Isla climbed into the loft. From down below, he shouted, 'We're going on an adventure!' It was a big mess up there, and the dust made her cough. All her stuff from

Easter Scout Camp was dumped on top of a pile of old coats and duvets.

'Found my tent,' she said, kicking away a pair of dead wasps. 'Here you go, our kid.'

Lac stood to one side as she chucked down the tent in its bag, landing with a clatter of poles.

'Sleeping bag.'

Chuck.

'And another one.'

Chuck.

'There's only one rucksack,' Isla called as she dropped it through the hatch. 'You'll have to have my school bag – it's pretty big.'

'Last thing now,' and a drawstring bag tumbled down the steps with a clunk.

In Lac's bedroom, Isla showed him her penknife and spork.

'That's a spoon with a spikey forky bit at the end of the round spoony bit.'

She pulled a couple of blue and black discs like small frisbees out of the bag.

'Look at these folding bowls.' Isla pushed the flat bottom of one to make the concertina sides open out. 'One each.'

Her voice came out as a squeak. Could they really pack up and leave the house where they'd lived for ever, just like that, and catch a train? Like Harry Potter travelling to Hogwarts the first time.

'Cool.' Lac grabbed a bowl and pushed it flat again.

She didn't tell him about a file on Mum's computer that didn't make sense. She couldn't get it out of her head. Inside a folder labelled 'Mac', an email addressed to Mum from 'National Public Order Intelligence Unit':

> Dear Madam, I am pleased to send you the findings of this investigation. Our review found that intelligence operations were not properly controlled. The report made recommendations to improve the control of undercover officers deployed to tackle criminality associated with public order and domestic extremism.

Sitting on Lac's bed, Isla chewed her thumbnail, wishing she understood what it meant. Was Mum in trouble?

Shaking her head, Isla said, 'Let's get packing. We're going on a mission: Find Mum.' She handed him her school bag. Lac whooped, and stuffed Luke Skywalker into the rucksack's side pocket. Isla wanted to call it Find Missing Mum but couldn't bear to say that word: missing. It reminded her of that 'missing persons' poster. *Have you seen her?*

In her bedroom she buried her nose in Weasley's fur.

'Please help us find her.'

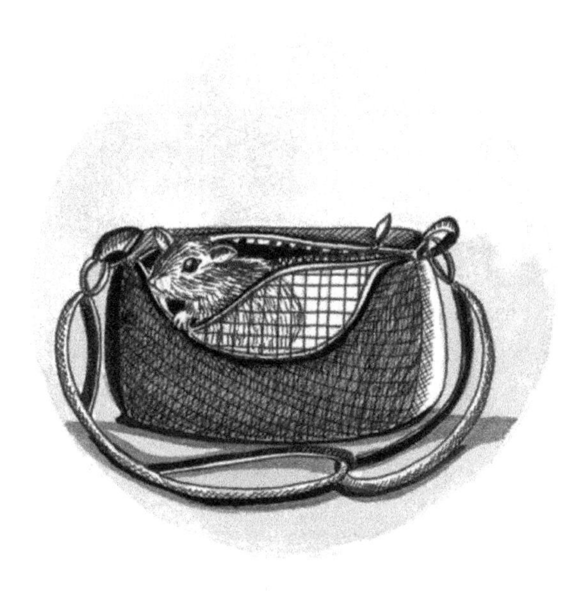

CHAPTER 6

JOURNEY

'Tickets please.'

The train guard shuffled closer and closer, squeezing past people standing in the aisle. Copying the smart woman opposite, Isla sat up straight. A bulge wiggled under the jacket on her lap. Absorbed in his tablet, her brother's lips moved with the characters zipping around in response to his fingers and thumbs. Luke Skywalker's head poked out of his pocket. Through the window, the outside world blurred as the whizzing train swayed and rocked from side to side.

'Sorry, sorry,' a lady said, her pregnant bump sticking out like a football, as she nearly fell onto their table. Isla felt dizzy. They were zooming away from home on a mission. Was this how astronauts feel when their rocket is launched?

As the guard glanced at the cracked screen on Isla's phone, hiccups started to bubble up in her throat.

'Where are your parents?' the guard asked.

Maybe she and Lac were more like spies pretending to be someone they weren't.

'In the next coach. We couldn't get seats together.'

The guard beeped the barcodes and moved on.

Isla pulled Weasley's carry bag from under her jacket, opened the zip and stroked the ginger fur on the back of his neck, where he liked it best. He'd eaten the little heap of hamster muesli she had tipped inside before they left home.

'Can you breathe alright in there, little buddy? Couldn't leave you behind. Wouldn't be fair to have an adventure without you. After all, the Hogwarts students are allowed to bring a pet.'

He nudged his nose into her palm, whiskers tickling as he nibbled a piece of bread she'd saved for him.

'Lovely nest you've made for yourself,' she said as she zipped the bag up again and kissed him through the front mesh.

Shoving her hand into her jeans pocket, her fingers scrabbled around until they found the silver ring that she'd swiped from Mum's box. Her middle finger slipped in and out, in and out, turning the cold metal warm. Lac fished a packet of Haribo out of his rucksack. Isla reached over and picked a fried egg out of the packet. Chomping the slurpy sweetness, the ring slipped loosely on her middle finger, and her fingertips slid over the corners and swirls of its pattern. *Please Mum, please come back.*

Isla pulled a piece of paper from her back pocket. She unfolded and refolded the note in her hands.

'Gone away for a few days. Please stay at Aunty Lou's. Sorry.'

She was gutted about missing the end of term concert. She was cross, too, that she couldn't go to the last climate strike of the term, because she and Kayla had been to all the others.

Isla hadn't expected Mum's reaction before the first strike. All the way home from school, she and Kayla had practised telling their parents, but when Isla said, 'Well I'm GOING!', Mum gave her a funny smile.

Leaning against the door frame between the living room and kitchen, Isla mumbled, 'You don't mind?'

Mum dunked one of her rank-smelling tea-bags in a mug. 'You're not going. You're too young, babs.'

'Don't call me babs. I'm not a baby anymore.' Isla felt like stamping her foot but that was babyish. 'This is serious. It's our future. Greta Thunberg says if all the kids go on strike, adults will have to take action, like reduce fossil fuels so there's less CO_2 in the air. She's on the news every day.'

'Telling us what a mess we made, the little madam.' Up and down, dunk, dunk.

'She's my hero.'

'Hero? Ha! No-one's going to save anything except themselves.'

'It's a crisis, Mum. You don't CARE about the planet. We're saving it. Fat lot of good you grown-ups did back in the day. It doesn't matter to you – you'll be dead.'

Mum hissed like she'd been burnt. She lifted out the tea bag and flipped it into the bin. She blew on the steaming mug. In the silence Isla could hear the kettle faintly fizzing.

She stared at the steam rising from her cup. 'Oh, we tried.' She sipped, with a little slurp, and blew again. 'You won't remember Dad going on protests. I first met him at a camp trying to close down a power station because of its carbon emissions. We took you on demonstrations when you were little.'

'You?' Isla shifted her feet.

'But I realised that family was more important.'

'For god's sake, Mum! More important than the end of the planet?'

'Yes.' She stood up and walked to the sink, adding cold water to her scalding brew.

'David Attenborough says it's a catastrophe.'

No response. She tipped up her cup and drank.

'Mum, you're spooking me. What's going on?'

'One day, Mac – went.'

'Went on a protest?'

'No. Went away. Never came back.' She gulped more tea.

'I know. The motorbike crash. But you're okay now, yeah?'

Mum sloshed the rest of her tea into the sink, turned and rested her hands on Isla's shoulders.

'I am okay, ducky. Thanks to you and the little devil. Which reminds me, he should be back from Aunty Lou's by now.'

Isla put her arms around her mum's waist. 'Why do we call her Aunty?'

'She's a really good friend. Not objecting, are you?'

'No, but...We've only got Uncle Dennis who we never see. Haven't we got any real aunties or uncles from Dad?'

'No.' She leant over the sink. Her long hair masked her face as she washed out her cup.

'Why did you call him Mac?'

'That was his name – Andy McCluskey.' She rinsed her cup again and again under the running water.

Isla bent forward and tried to look at her face behind the curtain of hair. 'McCluskey?'

'I meant MacLean.'

‘I thought he was called Sandy.’

‘That’s what I said.’ That was Mum all over. You could never trust what she said. Was she mixing Dad up with another boyfriend? Was she actually talking about Dad at all?

CHAPTER 7

SCOTLAND

Hours later, the guard walked through the train, announcing,

'We are now approaching Glasgow Central Station where this train terminates.' The guard threw a suspicious glance at the two youngsters whose parents had not appeared. 'Glasgow Central. All change, please. All change.'

Swept along in a sea of passengers flowing into the huge station hall, Isla checked Weasley's bag was hanging safely over her shoulder and grabbed Lac's hand. Crowds of tall people, coats swishing around their bodies, rushed past as if the children were invisible. Muffled loudspeaker announcements echoed in the cavernous space. '*Ding-dong*. The neff thren tae Ochnammmfn wull dip arut frm pla'frm eet, callin at ......'

Pigeons strutted and coo-ed on the shiny floor, one pecking at a half-chewed burger under a bench, nudging the box with its beak to get at the ketchup-y bread. More birds swooped down to join the feast, but the biggest one chased them away with a squawk and a flutter of wings. Isla laughed when Lac copied the birds' walk, head jerking forward on his neck in time with his stepping feet.

'Trrrrrill,' sang Lac, rolling his r's.

At the ticket office Isla couldn't understand the man behind the glass window when she asked where to get their next train.

'What did he say, Isla?'

'I think he said: "Just through the arcade, hen."' Isla stopped and looked around.

'What's a hen got to do with it?'

'I don't know.'

Lac half-walked, half-ran to keep up with her. When Isla asked a tall lady in red heels which way to go, she bent down and asked Lac,

'Are you all right, laddie?'

He sniffed and nodded.

'What's your name?'

'Lachlan MacLean.' Isla clamped her teeth. *Don't give away our secret.* Could she trust him not to blab about Mum?

'How old are you?'

'Eight.' He jerked his head towards Isla. 'I'm with my sister.'

'Are you sure you're okay?'

Lac pulled Luke Skywalker out of his pocket and made his toy nod to the lady.

A flock of pigeons flew up to the glass roof stretching high above their heads. 'Coo-oo-ooo' called Lac, tipping his head skywards. They found the platform and plopped down onto the train's seats with a bottle of orange pop to share. It was called Irn Bru.

Spotting a woman in uniform coming into their carriage, hiccups started rising in Isla's throat. She swallowed twice and fumbled for her phone. *Come on, Isla, you can do it.*

'Remember,' Isla whispered to Lac, 'the guard is like Darth Vader. Don't say a word. To her or anyone.'

The door screeched as it slid open, and the guard made straight for Isla and Lac.

'Tickets from Glasgow please.'

Isla held out her phone. She wished the screen wasn't cracked.

'How old are you?'

Lac put a Haribo cola bottle in his mouth and giggled.

'Sixteen,' she said, kicking Lac to remind him. *Be brave like Hermione Granger.* 'Our mum's meeting us at Oban.'

The guard looked at the ticket again, then back at her and Lac.

'I don't know what your game is – you're not sixteen. I'm calling the police. Children aren't allowed to travel alone.'

A woman wearing a red beret who was sitting across the aisle leant over.

'Don't worry, I'll take care of them. I'll hand them over to their mum.'

The train slowed down and as signs for a station came into view, the guard rushed down the carriage to open the doors. She called over her shoulder,

'All right. But I'll be keeping an eye on them.'

The woman winked and Isla smiled a thank you.

As the train hurtled through dense forest, Isla stared through the mesh at Weasley asleep in his nest. Yesterday this was an adventure, a game. Today it was deadly serious. Head drooping, her eyes closed.

That argument with Mum about the climate strikes had left a sour taste. Afterwards, Isla remembered how she used to sleep between Mum and Dad, cuddling SuperTed. If Lac asked about

Dad, she made up something about him throwing baby Lac in the air and catching him. Lac always said, 'I wish he never died.' And Isla would say, 'Me too.'

What had Mum said? Family was more important?

Isla hardly knew anything about Mum's life. Just the bare facts: her job at the hospital, her friend Lou, her smell and crushing hugs and awful clothes. Nana and Grandpa, Uncle Dennis and their cousins in Dudley. The raw spot that was Dad was off limits. Anytime Isla asked about him, Mum turned her face away and said, 'Please don't.' So she didn't ask.

You wouldn't think you could miss somebody who's been gone over half your life. But Isla did. Sometimes the emptiness made her grumpy. Once, she said to Kayla, 'At least you've got a dad.' But she never said it again. Sometimes a not-believing feeling swamped her. Writing those letters made her feel like he was there even when he wasn't. Sometimes Isla was angry. Stupid, stupid motorbike. If he hadn't had that bike, he'd still be here.

Mum couldn't stand her talking about Dad. There were no photos of him in the house. That was another thing Isla didn't understand about Mum.

And now she'd gone away – but Isla didn't know why. Or if she'd still be on the island when they got there.

It seemed like seconds later that the woman's voice woke her up.

'Here we are, kids,' she said, pulling her suitcase off the luggage rack above the seat. Outside the window a sign declared 'Fáilte don Oban.'

'Is this it?' Lac asked.

'Aye, this is Oban right enough. Any further and we'll end up in the sea.'

They climbed off the train and walked along the platform under the scrutiny of the guard.

'I can't see your mum anywhere.'

'Um, we're meeting her at the youth hostel,' Isla said in a rush.

The woman looked disgruntled. 'That's not very convenient. I only said I'd see you off the train.'

'Oh yes, that's fine. We know the way. Bye,' Isla said as they emerged from the station. She flung her head back and walked with long Hermione-like strides in the opposite direction to the woman.

'Thanks,' called Lac over his shoulder.

The Youth Hostel was easy to find.

'That white house across the harbour,' said the girl behind a stall selling candy floss and sweets.

Isla told the same story about meeting Mum to the adult in charge of the hostel, only this time Mum would be there when they arrived on the island tomorrow.

They bought chips, sat on the quay and fed Weasley some bits of carrot, staring at a massive ship with *Caledonian MacBrayne* painted in two-metre high letters on its side.

'Watch a seagull doesnae steal yer chups,' a boy said, rocking past on his skateboard.

'What did he say?' Lac asked.

'Something about a seagull stealing our chips.' Story of her life – not quite getting what people have said.

Lac looked up and spotted gulls flying everywhere, strutting on the quayside, swooping over the ship, and sitting on the rail of every boat. He danced around waving a chip at them before popping it in his mouth.

'Is there something strange about the way that boy spoke?' Isla asked.

Lac cocked his head.

'I mean, as if we've heard it before?'

Lac shrugged.

Isla shrank into her puffer jacket and stroked her hamster. She'd forgotten his water bottle, so she held his nose over a little puddle, but he tried to escape her hands and jump onto the chip paper.

'Uh-uh, no chips for you, buddy.' She dipped her fingers in the puddle and wet his nose and mouth, then zipped him back in his nest bag,

Fishing boats bobbed, their cables clinking against masts in the early evening light.

'We need to find a shop and buy some supplies for tomorrow,' she said. 'We can be like –' she fished around in her brain for ideas. 'Who is that stormtrooper who fights for survival?'

'Finn.'

'Like Finn.'

'He didn't go to the *shop*, duh!'

Isla twisted a strand of hair round her fingers, round and round, and stared at the water. *Don't cry.*

'No, but we're on an earth mission and might have to fight for our survival.'

'What? We've got no weapons,' he wailed. His trembling lip matched her beating heart.

'I mean we've got to stock up, take care of ourselves.' Isla looked into his eyes. 'We've got to be brave to accomplish our mission.'

Lac gave his sister the thumbs-up and they slapped a triumphant high-five. He slashed the air with Luke Skywalker's lightsaber.

CHAPTER 8

ABOARD SHIP

Isla's heart was still pounding when they set off early next morning, the sunrise painting the mountains behind them a pale yellow. The massive ship towered above the quayside. It was too early to try Mum's number again. A greasy stink filled the air, chains clanked and men in yellow jackets shouted at cars and lorries lined up ready to board. In the oily gap between the ship and the dock, transparent jellyfish floated under the water, menacing brown fronds drifting in the current.

'Yeuch! Disgusting!'

But her brother hadn't heard. His shoulders were shaking. His gaze was focused on the hulking grey ship and tears streamed down his face.

'What's wrong?'

Two lines of snot slid out of his nostrils. 'What if Mum was SHIPWRECKED?'

Isla's stomach lurched.

'A hundred percent, Mum has not been shipwrecked.'

'How do you know?'

'Ships don't sink these days. That was in olden times, in wars with pirates and cannonballs.' She couldn't think of anything else to say from her foggy brain.

'We didn't have breakfast.'

'We'll have beans on toast in a bit.' Isla's insides were knotted; she wasn't the least bit hungry.

They had to get on this ship.

The only sure thing was that Mum had boarded this same ship a few days ago. Surely she'd seen all Isla's missed calls? Isla didn't have a clue what was going on in Mum's head, but that was nothing new. Whenever she came home from work with slumped shoulders and crashed into the armchair, Isla would hang around in the kitchen, wishing Mum would talk to her. But usually, she'd just ask Isla to put the kettle on, and Isla would go upstairs and talk to Weasley, while downstairs Mum was sunk in her own world.

What if she was slumped like that now? She hadn't texted. That's why they were on her trail. Anything could have happened. What if she'd been kidnapped?

Isla and Lac sneaked in amongst a crowd of kids jostling and shoving towards the ship.

'Are we in a mystery?' Lac whispered as they shuffled up the gangplank.

'Yes.' *The Mystery of the Lost Mum,* she thought. 'I hope Luke Skywalker's up for some spying.'

'Luke Skywalker isn't a *spy.*'

'No, but Finn and Rose Tico were. Remember when they sneaked on a spaceship to find the tracker?' Lac made Luke nod his head.

'They were on an undercover mission, disguised as First Order officers.'

'But they were caught.'

'We won't be. Not us.'

They had to find her. They only had one mum, and no dad.

Safely aboard, vibrations from the engines filtered through their shoes and up their legs.

'Yessss,' Isla cried, punching the air. 'We did it again.'

'We're on a ship!' Lac shouted, running from window to window in a huge lounge, like a dog going berserk. 'A real ship.'

Isla jumped at the BOOM of two blasts of the ship's horn. 'Ding-dong' went the tinny loudspeaker. As usual, Isla couldn't make out the words.

'We're off now, hen,' an old man said sitting nearby. *Maybe 'hen' meant 'ducky'.*

Lac and Isla chased each other through the café and lounge, and outside to the deck. The engines throbbed, *Find Mum, find Mum, find Mum.* A mob of cawing gulls flew above two white lines of foam gushing behind the ship, and they watched the town and rocky shoreline becoming smaller as they headed out to sea.

'Will Mum be there on the island?'

'Yup.' *I hope so.*

Isla looked at the ring for the hundredth time, feeling the sharp corners of the cross and the smooth edge of the circle. She had to believe. *Please let Mum be there.* Sounded pathetic.

Lac balanced Luke Skywalker on the handrail. 'Will there be knights on the island? Doing missions.'

Isla burst out laughing. 'Of course not. They're just in stories.'

He picked at a patch of crusty seagull droppings on the railing.

'Will we have to kill any wild animals?'

Isla couldn't stop chuckling. 'No, you dumb-brain. It's just like England, except – well, it's Scotland. With beaches. No wild animals.' Isla didn't know that for sure.

'Beaches! I didn't pack my swim shorts.'

'You can swim in your pants.'

Lac squealed at the seagulls, 'We're going to play on the beach as well as do a mission.'

Looking at the huge expanse of sea, the ship lurching up and down over the waves made Isla feel sick.

'It's freezing out here. Let's go in.'

CHAPTER 9

ISLAND

'Wake up.' Isla shook Lac. His eyes popped open in an instant and he jiggled Luke Skywalker up and down.

'Ready for adventure, Luke?'

Groups of passengers were packing away their iPads and half-eaten packets of biscuits. Lac squirmed as Isla dragged her hairbrush through his bushy ginger curls, so unlike her and Mum's long black hair.

None of the adults saw little Lac squashed between a sea of enormous rucksacks as they followed the gang of girls and boys down a sloping ramp and along a pier to the shore. Sunshine glinted on a sign: Fáilte do Mora. Isla noticed a stone cross with names of soldiers carved into its plinth that was just like the war memorial in the park at home. Except the cross on this one was surrounded by a circle – just like Mum's ring. Strange. It even had the same swirly patterns.

She bent down and zipped up Lac's jacket. 'Not a word, remember.'

'About our mission?'

'About anything. Don't open your mouth.'

'Is it a secret mission?'

'Yes.' Isla twisted the ring in her pocket, tracing its pattern with her finger. 'I mean it. Promise not to open your mouth?'

He opened it and wobbled his front tooth with his tongue.

'Ergh, gross.'

He beckoned with his finger, and she bent down.

'We're hungry,' he whispered into her ear, shoving Luke Skywalker's head beside his lips.

Isla gave him a packet of yogurt raisins from her bag.

The school party clambered aboard a minibus and drove off. A woman walked forward, wearing the same worried expression as Mum, deep grooves carved between her eyebrows. But it wasn't her. Lac's face crumpled.

'I'll call her, just in case she picks up,' Isla said.

'I'm sorry caller, we are unable to connect you.' Same old. How many times had she heard that message? It felt like there was a stone in her stomach. Isla texted,

it's me we're here on mora pls txt bk xxxxx

Willing her voice not to wobble, Isla said, 'I told you Mum wouldn't be here. That was just a story I told the youth hostel man, so he wouldn't figure out our secret.'

His eyes flashed at her. 'You lied.'

'I had to.'

'You could be lying about shipwrecks.'

Isla couldn't look at him.

A cold breeze swirled around Isla's face and neck, and a half-familiar smell reminded her of something. She opened her coat so that Weasley could sniff the sharp air. Three seagulls flew in circles above them.

'*Squew-squew-squew*,' they called.

'Squew-squew-squew,' Lac said back to them.

Two hoots from the ship blasted out, and it slid away leaving a thick oily streak floating on the sea. On their right a beach curved away into the distance. A ruined church tower overlooked gravestones poking up behind a wall. Isla humped her rucksack onto her back.

'Task One of our mission is to set up camp.' It was weird, being scared and sad and excited all at the same time. She rubbed her nose to get rid of that funny smell.

'*Squew!*' the seagull said.

'Squew,' Lac said.

'Ip-dip-doo, the cat's got the flu, the monkey's got the chicken pox so out goes you.' Isla's right fist fell away, and she raised her left arm.

'That-a-way.' Isla was pretending she knew where to go. She turned her back on the sun and let it warm her neck.

The road led up from the harbour to a cluster of white cottages in front of a grassy mound. They plodded past a blue 'Toilets' sign and a snack van advertising crab sandwiches – *yuk*. A board announcing fishing trips pictured a grinning bald man cradling an enormous dead fish in his arms as if it were a baby. *Gross.*

'This is further than it looked,' Isla said, puffing up the slope. *And it might be the wrong way*. Behind a fence, a pale brown cow stared at them through a shaggy fringe of hair, its tail flicking flies away from a backside encrusted with dried poo. They walked past a shop and arrived at the green stretch of land in front of the cottages.

Lac dropped his rucksack from his shoulders and dragged it along the ground, his face creased in a furious expression. He hadn't uttered a word as he soldiered under his heavy load, but now he made a pathetic mewing sound.

'Stop grizzling,' Isla said. It was too big for him, but what could she do? No good turning up without a sleeping bag. Isla felt horrible about being mean to him, even if he was annoying. After all, it was his mum, too, who was lost. Trying to be clever like Hermione wasn't working. Mainly because Hermione was a witch and could use magic to help her do things, whereas Isla was an ordinary Muggle.

She wiped away her tears and pointed to a small dip. 'Over there.' She helped Lac hoist the pack onto his back and forced her feet forwards.

Isla heaved the rucksack off her burning shoulders. From down here they couldn't see the cottages. About a hundred metres in front of them the sloping grass turned into rocks, which dropped onto a sandy beach. A line of black seaweed ran the length of the beach, marking a boundary: on one side the sand was hard and wet, and on the other it was soft and white. Isla guessed that ridged ripples in the wet sand showed where the sea had been and gone.

'Just like our problem,' Isla said to herself. 'Mum was there with us at home and now she's gone.'

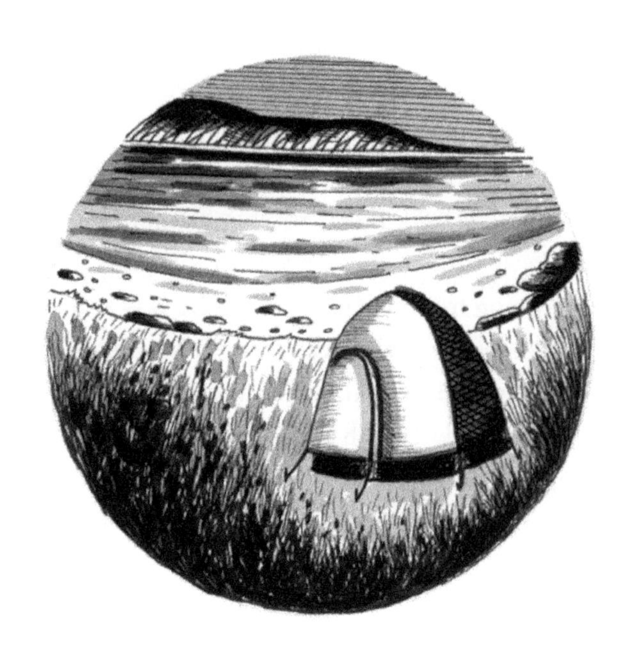

CHAPTER 10

CAMP

They lugged their bags to a flat spot. Kicking dried up lumps of sheep's doo-doo out of the way, Isla laid out the tent and inserted bendy poles into their slots, just like she'd learned at Scout Camp. While she tried to remember what to do next, Lac crawled under the floppy canvas, and lifted it upright.

'Genius! That's how it goes,' Isla said. It all came back to her: poles then pegs. The wind tried to stop them, but together they forced the pole ends into their grommets, and Lac held them tight while Isla stuck pegs in the ground.

They high-fived each other in front of the tent, which was leaning sideways but upright. 'It's sort of right. Yay for Scout Camp.' Lac pulled the door zip, and they wriggled inside and slipped into their unrolled sleeping bags, curling up together with Weasley in the middle.

Isla was dreaming about a police car whizzing round the corner, but its siren only made a teeny tinny sound. Her hand swiped a tickly place on the back of her neck. It still tickled. Isla rubbed again, and it crawled up around her ear, over her earlobe. '*Eeeeeeeeeeeee.*' A high-pitched whine zapped straight to her eardrum. Isla screamed and slapped the side of her head, but the fly danced away to the top of the tent.

'Weasley! Get it! Why couldn't it screech in my deaf ear?'

It was still light. Next to her, Lac yawned.

'Mew,' he whimpered, tapping his tummy.

Isla rolled over and rubbed her eyes.

'I'm starving.' A groan escaped from her throat. 'Oh no.'

She remembered where they were.

A strong wind was rocking the sides of the tent. Tears flooded her kid brother's eyes. Isla knew he was thinking: *Can we find Mum now?* Isla pulled the purse from the side pocket of her rucksack and slipped out two ten-pound notes. Peering inside, she checked the credit card was still there. She didn't feel bad about raiding the emergency stash, seeing as she was buying food, which was Mum's job.

'Let's go to the shop,' she said. 'We need something to eat. We can ask there if they've seen Mum.' She sprinkled some flakes and seeds into Weasley's nest and slipped him back inside, but left the bag open.

Lac made little 'peep-peep' noises and pulled on his trainers. As soon as Isla unzipped the tent, he grabbed Luke Skywalker and rolled out onto the grass, fighting fiercely with Luke against their foe. Isla straightened her top, yanked up her skinny jeans, brushed her hair, and zipped up the tent so Weasley wouldn't escape.

'Ready for action, Action Man?'

Lac gave her a scornful look.

'Remember, don't say a word.'

Inside the little supermarket they trailed up and down the aisles and Isla filled their basket with bread rolls, two bottles of pop, a tin of tuna, ham, cheese-strings, crisps, an apple for Weasley and two chocolate bars. In the queue, Isla prayed to be served by the woman who looked the same age as Mum, not the lad with long ginger hair. Isla shivered at the picture on his black tee shirt: an owl and skull hovering above the words *Fowl Youth* in gothic writing. He'd probably be as much help as horrible Ally. Isla cringed inside as she remembered. *A reject like you.*

The shop lady was scanning items from another customer's basket.

'Awful windy today,' she said.

'Could be a storm brewing,' answered her customer as the till beeped and she packed her plastic bag.

Something about the way they spoke jogged a feeling in Isla, a *knowing* kind of sense at the back of her mind. She passed her basket to the woman.

'Nine pounds forty.'

Isla fumbled in her pocket, her heart hammering, and handed over the ten-pound note. Giving her the change, the lady said,

'Is there anything else I can help you with?'

A feeling of relief washed over her.

'Yes.' Isla stood tall and put on a grown-up voice. 'My brother and I are camping here. We said we'd meet our mother but –' *did it sound fake?* '– there's no signal where she is so we can't call and say we've arrived.'

'That's strange,' the lady replied. 'We usually have a good signal all over the island.'

'We're from Birmingham. Maybe that's why.'

Sounded pathetic. Isla swallowed. 'So, er, have you seen her? A bit taller than me, larger, you know, body,' – Isla held her arms out around her chest and middle – 'blue glasses, long black hair.'

'English?'

'Yes.' *What else would she be?*

She sat on the stool behind her.

'Archie, have you served an English lady like this wee girl's telling us?' she asked the long-haired teenager.

'Loads,' he said, without breaking the flow of scanning his customer's shopping, each one beeping before he placed it in the bagging area.

'We've had a lot of visitors this summer,' the lady said with a shrug.

'We'll be okay,' Isla said. 'I mean, she just said she'd call in to our camp sometime. We're fine, we don't need her or anything.'

The shop lady's eyebrows squidged together into a frown. A lipstick smudge appeared at the corners of her mouth as she opened it again. 'I thought you said you were looking for her.'

'Yes, we are. Just to say hello really.' Isla tried to sound casual, but her palms were sticky, and her tongue felt too big for her mouth. The shop's shutter rattled and banged in the wind, and a car door slammed.

'Where did you say she's staying?' She looked at her over her glasses.

'Umm, not sure.'

'A cottage?' Her eyes narrowed like Mrs Karim in her office after that fight.

'Maybe.' Isla coughed, cleared her throat. 'Probably,' she said in a louder voice.

'Or the hotel? You could try the Hebridean Inn.' Her eyes looked extra-large through the lenses in her glasses.

'No, I don't think a hotel.' Isla glanced towards the door and slipped her finger in and out of Mum's ring in her pocket. Newspapers and empty boxes skittered across the car park outside.

Archie served another customer, finishing with the usual 'Is there anything else I can help you with?'

The way he said you – 'yoo' – Isla had heard that before somewhere.

'There's so many cottages just now,' the lady said. Her face broke into a smile. 'There's a visitor centre four miles yonder. Easy to find. Follow this road between the beach and the machair, turn left along the loch by Island House – '

'– where they used to hang people,' Archie said behind his curtain of hair, which was the same rusty-red as Lac's. Isla blinked; had the owl on his tee-shirt winked?

Why were these people so confusing? Isla couldn't go to the machair because she didn't know what it was. She didn't like that boy, either. He was creepy.

'I'm sure they'll be able to help,' the lady said, ignoring him.

'Thanks,' Isla said, turning to go. The automatic door slid open.

'Your Mum,' Archie said. 'Does she talk like you?' *Yoo.*

Her bag bashed against the door. 'Yes,' Isla said over her shoulder.

Of course.

They trudged back to the tent, kicked off their trainers, and stuffed their mouths full of ham and bread rolls washed down with pop, followed by sweets. Isla tipped some water into an upturned bottle top and placed it carefully in Weasley's nest. Lac chucked his empty bottle on the grass.

'Hey,' Isla shouted, 'no rubbish! It's bad enough buying plastic bottles, don't make it worse.' He crawled over the grass and threw it back at her. Isla picked a long stalk of grass, poked it between her front teeth, and sucked. It tasted sour. Not a great start as a detective.

When Weasley's pink tongue had finished lapping water, Isla picked him up. His whiskers tickled as he nibbled a piece of apple and some seeds in her palm. She stroked his neck and burrowed her nose into his ginger fur. It reminded her of nuzzling Dad's beard. She whispered into his ear. 'There's something spooky about that boy, Archie.'

Lac was fixing Luke Skywalker's lightsaber into the plastic hand.

'I'm going back to the shop,' Isla said. She popped the hamster back inside the tent. 'We need water. And I'll ask more questions. Will you be okay on your own? Just five minutes?'

He nodded, picking at little tufts of grass between his knees and making a heap.

'Get back in the tent if it's too windy.' Isla walked off up the slope, bending her head against the wind. In the shop she picked up a large bottle of water, some milk, pouches of Nesquik and a packet of Hobnobs.

At the front of the queue, a woman in a red *Royal Mail* jacket packed away her shopping.

'Marshin leave,' the postwoman said.

'Marshin leave en draster,' the shop lady said as the customer left the shop.

'You all right, lovey?' the smiley lady asked when Isla put their basket on the counter. *No, Isla thought. Mum might have been shipwrecked but I don't dare ask if you've heard anything about boats sinking.*

Isla mumbled, 'Fine, thanks.' She pointed to the doorway. 'How come I couldn't get what you were saying to that lady?'

'We were chatting in garlic.'

'Garlic?'

The boy on the other till sniggered. Just like Ally.

'We were talking our language of the islands,' the lady said.

'Not English?'

'No, we speak both English and Garlic. Like the Irish.'

'I thought Irish people speak Gaelic,' Isla said.

The boy snorted again. 'It's Gallic.'

The shopkeeper pulled Isla's basket towards her. 'Aye, that's what I said,' she replied, scanning Isla's shopping with a series of beeps. 'Is it just these things, hen?'

'Yes please.' Isla produced the credit card *for emergencies only*. The lady's eyes flicked from the card to her.

'Is this your card?'

Isla looked out of the door, and down at her feet.

'Umm, it's my Mum's.'

'Sorry, hen, I'll need to see your ID. Not driving licence, I can see you're too young. School bus pass?'

Isla shook her head.

'Birth certificate's no good I suppose?'

'No.'

'I can't take the card without your Mum. You'll have to pay cash.'

Isla fished another ten-pound note from her pocket.

'Are you *sure* you're okay, darling?' the lady said, as she handed over the change.

Isla dipped her head.

'Surely your ma will come for you today?'

'Yes, she'll be here any minute.' Isla grabbed her bag and bolted out of the shop.

CHAPTER 11

LOST BOY

Isla pelted to the tent. She'd been longer than five minutes and an uneasy feeling was creeping up her spine. Harsh gusts of wind blew in her face when she called Lac's name. A dozen black and white seagulls circled above her, crying their penetrating '*Squew-uew-uew*' calls. There was no answering shout from Lac. Just the whoosh of the wind and the gulls' cries. One swooped to the rocks, its orange beak like a spear, and launched upwards again with a piercing '*pee-ee-eep*'. It sounded like a warning.

The tent was unzipped, empty. Near the entrance, Weasley was gnawing at a bit of dried seaweed. A Bounty wrapper and the empty pop bottle had blown inside, and Isla looked around to tell Lac off about the rubbish. He wasn't on the grass where she'd left him. Isla dropped her bag, laid Weasley on her sleeping bag, and zipped up the tent. Lac didn't jump out at her from behind the tent, and there was nowhere else to hide, if he was waiting to ambush her.

Maybe he'd fallen asleep again. Isla circled the tent one more time, hoping to trip over his snoozing body.

Body. What if –? A shiver shot through her arms and legs. Isla shouted, but gusts of wind carried her feeble voice away. She tried again, yelled with her mouth jammed open as wide as she could, her head thrown back and arms rigid by her side, fists thrust downwards.

'La-a-a-a-a-ac!' Her shout disappeared into the wind.

Taking a huge gasp of air, she screamed his name again, turning round and round in case he emerged from a hole in the ground or a hidden cave.

'La-a-a-a-a-ac!'

Maybe he'd gone for a pee. Isla raced to the toilet block, banged through the boys' door and stood stock still. Empty. Just a revolting smell and a leaking pipe going *drip-drip* into a puddle on the concrete floor.

Her hair flew into a jumbled tangle over her face as she zigzagged towards the shore, screaming 'Lac! Lac!' over and over again.

No, Isla told herself. She twisted away from the sea, turned her back on the awful thought. *No, not – can't be, must be somewhere, not in – where?*

A group of sheep watched her from the safety of a mossy hillock.

'Where *is* he?' Isla wailed.

A brown Labrador dog bounded up, sniffing her feet. Behind him, a man wearing wellies and a coat blotched with green stains puffed up the slope, pushing hard on a long stick.

'What's up, hen?' he asked. Isla jumped, shrank backwards. The dog licked her hand.

'Don't mind Percy,' he said. 'He won't bite. He likes you.'

It was the man who frightened her, not the dog, but Isla knew it was dangerous to say so. She planted her feet firmly apart. She couldn't run away. She had no choice, she had to speak to him. Percy circled round her legs, snuffling and licking. He shook his whole body, spraying drops all over Isla.

'My brother. He's gone. I can't find him.'

The man leant on his stick. When he spoke, the flesh under his chin wobbled.

'Little lad? Red and blue hoody?'

Isla nodded, looked up at him from blinking eyes, her jaw quivering. *If he's a villain, I'm toast.* Percy jumped around in circles, crouched and leapt, pleading for a game.

The man pointed. 'He's down in the cove yonder.'

A tinny ringing sound filled her ears. 'The c-cove?' Isla was already crying for a small lifeless body, face down, dumped by an unforgiving sea.

'Aye,' he replied. 'Percy and me helped him, so we did, digging a fortress for Luke Skywalker. Grand little lad.'

Isla stared at him, and raced off at supersonic speed, shouting, 'Thanks!' over her shoulder. She hot-footed up the rise. At the top, she looked down on a tiny beach where two canoes lay stranded side by side, and plastic bottles ditched by the tide were strewn along the shore.

And her dumb-ass kid brother, scooping sand onto a large mound, topped by Luke Skywalker.

'Lac!' Isla screamed, plunging down the dune, tripping on the tufts of spiky grass, the wind whipping up sprays of sand which stung her cheeks.

Isla fell and landed on her knees next to him. Pulling him into a massive hug, she cried harsh sobs that shook them both and squeezed him tight. She wanted to crush his bones, to make him part of her so that he'd never face danger again. Her sobbing gave way to lurching hiccups which jolted through their joined-up bodies.

Finally, he broke free, shoving her away with a red face. Rubbing his squashed nose, he scowled.

Isla seized his shoulders. 'Don't *ever* do that again.'

She squeezed his arms.

'Don't *ever ever* go off like that,' she repeated.

Seagulls circled in the reflection of his scared green eyes.

'I thought you were *dead.*'

Isla sat on the beach, hugging her knees.

'Sorry, our kid,' she said. 'I thought I'd lost you as well as Mum.'

Silence. No reply. He turned away from her, looked at his sandcastle, and planted Luke Skywalker more firmly as Lord of his territory. He opened his mouth.

'Craaaarkk!'

Isla pushed the hair out of her eyes and did a double take. There was a gap in his grin. With his thumb and forefinger, he pulled a little white tooth from his pocket and displayed it on his open palm. He closed his fist and went back to digging with a grimy piece of plastic bottle.

Picking up a fistful of soft sand, Isla opened her hand and the tiny grains dribbled through her fingers. Her nose wrinkled. That smell again. Kind of whiffy, old, not horrible but not nice either. Isla pulled the ring out of her pocket and rolled it around in her palm. Stroking the pattern felt comforting. A strange feeling swept into her head. What if the ring held a secret code? The circle round the cross, decorated with under-and-over loops going round and round, meeting each other in a continuous pattern. Like a thread, interlocking but also separate. Did it have a special connection with this island?

In the sky, a crowd of seagulls were going bananas, brown birds attacking the white gulls. Up high a massive sunlit cloud looking like a dragon erupted a stretch of fiery vapour from a scaly snout. Her ear tingled. When Isla touched it, she drew a sharp breath of pain, and saw blood on her finger. She felt it again. No stud. She must have lost her ear-ring when she fell. Just as well it wasn't the other ear. She fingered her zinger and gently pushed the earpiece – it was firmly in place.

A strange yellow light covered everything around them, and rays of silver beamed down from behind the clouds onto the foaming sea. Over by the rocks, the waves had transformed from gentle swashing to crashing and spitting columns of spray. A fishing boat was ploughing through the sea, its front rising and falling in time with the waves.

Coo-ing and croaking noises from Lac's game with Luke filtered through the air. Grains of sand grated on her teeth as Isla put her fist in her mouth to stop herself crying. Silently, she pleaded *Give me back my Mum*.

Another handful of sand sifted slowly through her fingers.

Isla picked at a worm-shaped heap of sand, wondering what was going on underneath, and smoothed it flat. Hopefully, she hadn't ruined the worm's home. She shivered. She knew nothing about worms. Isla heard Ally's sneering voice: *You don't know nothin.*

That was the problem.

CHAPTER 12

WHERE'S WEASLEY?

Back at the camp, Isla crammed their belongings into the rucksacks. How would Hermione Granger have dealt with the shop lady? A swirl of angry wind made her hair fly all over the place. Lac tapped her on the shoulder. He was speaking on her deaf side, and she couldn't hear anything above the rushing noise of the wind.

'Aaaaarwrkk?'

'We've got to get out of here. I think the shop lady suspects us. If she calls the police, we're done for. We won't complete our mission and we'll never find Mum.'

Lac ran to the rocks for a pee and waved at each sheep he passed on the way back, singing 'Chirrup-ee-wee' at the ones that lifted their heads. He bent to lift his bag.

'Wait!' Isla knelt back on her heels with the nest bag in her hands.

'Where's Weasley?'

She reached all around the empty tent , her fingers searching for fur, but felt only smooth plastic. She jumped up and looked around.

'Weasley's gone!'

Lac snapped his head up. Isla patted the grass.

'Weasley, Weeeeeeasley,' she called in her softest voice.

Lac poked a stick underneath a pile of dead seaweed and skittered a few metres to peer into a sandy dip on his hands and knees.

'Weeeeeeeeasley,' Isla called into the wind, running back up the slope. 'Come on Weasley-boy, chuckie chuckie.' *Isla, he's not a chicken*, she told herself.

She tugged at a knot in her hair. With a painful jerk, several strands came away in her fingers. Through her tears, Isla felt Lac wrap his arms around her middle and lay his head on her chest.

'Weasley's MISSING. He must have bolted. He could be anywhere.' Isla hiccupped. 'He could be – "

Tears streaked down Lac's face.

'– dead.' The awful word fell between them like a stone. She pulled away from Lac. 'What are we going to DO?'

She put her head in her hands. How could she expect an eight-year-old kid to come up with answers? Hermione had two friends her own age when she was in detective mode. Ally's mocking voice echoed in her head again: *You don't know what to do,* and her horrible sneering tone, *Mummeee!* Isla pulled out the tent pegs and poles and did her best to roll it up, then secured the bundle to her pack and closed the top opening. She scanned the empty space where the tent had been.

Isla humped the rucksack onto her sore shoulders and searched the area of their camp one last time.

'We've got to go.'

'Squew, quew, quew?' sang Lac.

'I don't know. That way.'

Isla pointed to the right, where the bay curved beyond the pier and the sandy shore became smaller as it receded into the distance. She shared out two biscuits each, and they crunched as they tramped across the springy grass, bent against the wind. Her eyes swept the area like a radar scanner, but nothing moved. 'I can't believe we've lost Weasley.' She kept shaking her head from side to side, as if that would cancel out the truth.

Remembering the shopkeeper, she looked back but couldn't see anyone watching them. *It's just the pop making my tummy gurgle,* she told herself, but her knees felt wobbly. Lac was waiting at the edge of the grassy area, which gave way to the beach a metre below.

'Can't jump down onto the sand with these heavy packs,' Isla said, so they lowered themselves backwards like astronauts landing on the moon.

Walking along the shore, the stink of rotting seaweed made Isla breathe through her mouth. It was the same smell she recognised when they stepped off the boat yesterday. An image flashed into her head. A beach. Holding Dad's huge hand. Funny smell. She pocketed a few shells that glistened like jewels on the sand.

They stopped for a rest and unwrapped a couple of cheese-strings. When Isla shouldered her pack again, there was a rustling behind her neck. It sounded like insects were crawling around her collar and she brushed them away.

Lac darted ahead on tiptoes, following bird tracks. That rustling sound was still there, sounding like a grasshopper was caught in her hair. She took out her zinger and flicked the tubing; maybe some moisture had got in. But the noise like static interference carried on.

Lac stopped, pointing at a dried-up starfish on the sand. Isla bent and touched it with her fingertip. As she tried to straighten up again, she staggered under the weight of her pack and keeled over onto the sand.

'Flippin Nora,' she yelled.

Lac crouched behind Isla to help her wriggle out of the arm loops. Whistling through the gap in his teeth, he started fumbling in the top pocket of her rucksack.

'Hey, leave my stuff alone.'

He stood up, cradling something in both his hands.

'Coo-oo,' he said, lifting closed palms to his face.

Isla's brain took a moment to click.

'Weasley! Was that you hissing? I thought it was interference from the wind on my zinger.'

Lac opened his fingers and Isla scooped up the furry bundle, holding him high above her head. 'How did you sneak in there?' she yelled. She shook him. 'I could have squashed you.' She shook his little body again.

He squeaked.

'Sorry, sorry.' She stuck her nose into his fur, then slung the nest bag over her shoulder and slipped him back inside.

'Don't try and get out. Or else.'

Thank goodness she'd found him and he hadn't died when she fell. Isla needed him with her on their mission to find Mum.

CHAPTER 13

ROCK POOL

As they walked, the tide crept up the beach, gradually nudging them across a line of dried seaweed and onto softer sand. They pitched the tent on a patch of grass beyond the pier just where it joined the beach. A tall, pointed rock towered over them, its bulk protecting them from the blustery wind blowing up from the sea.

Several metres away, the incoming waves had created a deep pool. Up and down, a patch of sea surged through a narrow gap in the rocks, making a sucking noise as it retreated. Lac kicked off his shoes and socks, hopped onto the beach and clambered over smooth rocks towards the pool, Luke Skywalker in his hand.

Isla sat on a flat rock and released Weasley from captivity in her rucksack. He jumped out of her open hands and snuffled around her feet. Unwrapping some chocolate, she recalled the warning in Oban about seagulls snatching their chips. Would a seagull want to snatch Weasley? She was relieved when she held out a piece of apple and called him, and he scurried back to her.

"You little sausage! Your nose is all sandy." She brushed off as much sand as she could and he nestled on her shoulder.

Isla bit a chunk off her chocolate bar. She remembered Ally's taunts of '*Mummee*', as if Isla was a baby who couldn't do anything without her mum. Well, she was carrying out this mission without Mum, and they were doing okay so far.

Isla flapped her arms at a cloud of insects bobbing around her head.

'Stop mithering me.'

Behind their spot, the sun shone red on a line of cliffs towering above scrubby slopes. How could they find out if Mum was out there somewhere? Isla realised that getting here was the easy part of the mission. She scratched her ankle, while a bird tweeted like crazy. *What's a blackbird doing on the beach?* Turned out it was Lac, cheeping as he hopped around the pool, making Luke carry out daredevil dives into the water. She ate the rest of the chocolate.

If Kayla was here, they'd at least have some ideas. She pulled out her phone and looked at Kayla's last text, and Isla's lies in reply.

K: *Didn't know u were goin to aunty*

I: Got to cos Mum's ill

K: *wen u back?*

I: dunno will msg u.

Isla's finger hovered over the ring button, but – no, she couldn't. Kayla would tell her mum and dad, then she and Lac would get carted away, which meant they'd never find Mum. She slipped the phone back in her pocket and –

'Eyyy, ergghh!' Isla spluttered. A cascade of water splurged down her face.

Lac ran off, sniggering. He'd emptied an old coffee cup full of sea water on her head, splashing Weasley too, and his sharp teeth stabbed her neck.

"Ouch!" She snatched him away, holding him at arm's length, his fur clumped in a sodden mess. Isla stowed him in his nest, and pushed strands of wet hair out of her face and licked her lips.

'Eeugh, it's disgusting.'

Lac was down at the rock pool, refilling.

'You idiot! My zinger!' She hooked it out from behind her ear and opened the battery compartment. Looked okay. Her fingers explored the side of her head. All dry, so she re-fixed the hearing aid in place. She scrambled to her feet and chased her brother to the rock pool. 'I'll get you.'

Lac jumped from one foot to the other in a 'can't get me' attitude, and sang, 'Chirrup-ee-wee, chirrup-ee-wee.'

Isla scrunched her face into an angry frown but couldn't help a loud cackle bursting out. 'You monster.'

'Cheepity-cheep,' pronounced Lac.

He hopped onto a rock in the middle of the pool, and – splash – one leg slipped into the water. The laugh gurgling in Isla's throat faded as he fell sideways and – crack – his head banged the rock. Like slow motion, his body rolled down and into the pool. Under the water.

His head broke the surface, coughing and gasping. He tried to stand up but slipped on the wet rock and fell back in, his hands sliding down the smooth stone. It happened again. And again. Isla leant over the edge and stretched out her arm. Lac wriggled like a stranded dolphin, straining to reach her open fingers. With a great effort, his hand grasped hers, and she hauled him out of the pool. He sat on the rock with heaving shoulders, spitting, coughing and shaking his head like a cat that's come in out of the rain.

'Jeez, our kid, you scared me. Are you okay?'

Isla slapped him on the back, and he coughed and burped. He winced when she pulled down her sleeve and pressed the cuff against a scrape which was oozing blood on his elbow. His cheek gleamed red with a graze.

'Let me look at your head.'

He turned his face to one side and screeched when Isla touched his ear which glowed deep crimson. It was boiling hot. He shivered in the wind.

He gave Isla a frightened look and a little 'mew' came from his lips.

'Let's get you out of these wet clothes.'

Isla helped him pull off his trainers and socks, jeans and t-shirt, bundled them under her arm, and headed back to the tent. Just in his underpants, Lac limped to the pool's edge and pulled out Luke Skywalker, who lay face down in the water.

Isla turned back into the wind. 'Come *on,*' she called over her shoulder.

Lac hobbled after her. At the tent, she struggled against the wind to help Lac into dry trackie bottoms. Weasley squeaked from his nest, trembling and sniffing through the mesh.

'Didn't bring any plasters,' Isla said. 'Still, salt is good for wounds, so sea water will help.'

'Cheep-cheep,' Lac complained when she dabbed his elbow with the wet t-shirt.

Isla laid out Lac's clothes on the grass to dry, but strong gusts blew them into an untidy heap. He looked scruffy and miserable, so she tipped a Nesquik pouch into the empty milk bottle, added fresh milk, and shook it up and down until it was brown and bubbly. They passed the bottle back and forth between them, wiping froth from their lips like grown-up beer drinkers. Isla poured a little water into the milk bottle top, which Weasley lapped with his tiny tongue.

Lac upended the bottle, drank and burped.

'Krrrrr, krrrrr,' he trilled, a chocolatey smear mingling with the graze on his cheek.

'Better now? Enough of the birdsong, and enough playing. We need a plan to find Mum. And we need food.'

CHAPTER 14

BRAIN FOOD

Salty wind lashed their faces and white tips capped the choppy waves out at sea. As soon as Isla and Lac sat behind the tent to shelter from the wind, those tiny black insects reappeared, swarming around them. Isla tipped the food stash out of her rucksack and scrabbled inside the pocket for her spork.

'Scran's up!'

'Craaark!'

The tin of tuna opened with a pop. Isla couldn't be mithered to find the bowls. She dug her spork into the moist flakes, ate a mouthful, gouged out a small chunk for Weasley and passed the tin to Lac. They had to wave their arms about to stop the mini-flies invading the food. He loaded a spork-ful into his wide-open mouth and passed the tin back.

'D'you remember Mum saying fish is brain food?'

He nodded. He was trying to persuade creepy-crawlies to walk over his finger.

'We need our brains, kiddo, so eat up.' She passed the tin back to him.

He chewed. Isla flapped her arms in front of her face and around her head.

She reached out her arm. 'Pass the crisps.' After the crisps they started on biscuits, followed by a swig of milk.

'Now, where are we up to on our mission?'

Isla picked a handful of pink flowers and put one on the ground between them.

'Number one: Mum came to this island.'

Thumbs-up sign from Lac, sitting cross-legged, eyes wide, as if he was on the carpet at school before a story. Weasley hunched next to him, nibbling grass.

She laid the next flower down. 'Two. She's here somewhere so we're going to look for her.'

Lac sat in his good boy pose, perfectly still. Isla didn't say out loud, *unless she's been and gone, and we've missed her.*

Another pink flower joined the other two. 'Three, be careful around adults who might stop us.'

Lac jerked his chin and cocked his head, asking a silent question.

'Adults don't think us kids can look after ourselves. They'd make us live with strangers called foster parents. Then we'd never find Mum.'

His eyes widened in alarm.

'But we can do it, can't we kiddo?'

His head joggled up and down loads of times, very fast.

'We're gonna do it! We're gonna find Mum!' Isla pounded her fist on the grass, scattering the flowers. She took another swig of milk, then stood up and waved her arms and body like a windmill.

'Phergh! These pests are getting everywhere – they're all in my hair.'

She checked her phone. 20:03. It was still light. A pink flower poked out of Weasley's mouth.

'Let's get inside. It's your bedtime, anyway.' As they crawled to the front of the tent, the fierce gusts in their faces seemed to blow the flies away.

'Go and pee by that rock, little 'un, and I'll get your toothbrush ready.'

He used the empty milk bottle as a water mug to brush his teeth.

'That's it, warrior,' Isla said. 'You're getting the hang of it.'

In his sleeping bag, they snuggled up with Weasley, and Isla told Lac his favourite story about the bear in the forest. He was asleep before the bear cub found its mother.

Isla unzipped a small hole in the tent door and poked her head out. The insects had definitely gone. She crawled out and sat with her hood up, staring at rose-coloured clouds. Hugging herself, she couldn't stop shivering. Dotted around on the grass, several massive podgy lambs nestled up against their mother sheep. *It's not fair.* Isla yearned to be sunk into a warm and cosy huddle.

Scrolling on her phone she googled 'public order intelligence' and found a load of stuff about a 'police officer working undercover' and, further down, an article about 'six protesters arrested demonstrating at a power station in 2010.' Mum had said she met Dad protesting at a power station.

Isla couldn't stop scratching an insect bite on her ankle. *Skrr-skrr-skrr.* Ouch! A bead of blood popped out of a tiny crater in the red lump like a micro-volcano. Despite the pain, it still itched.

She googled 'undercover': *'Undercover, adj; involving secret work within a community or organization, especially for the purpose of police investigation or espionage.'* Espionage meant spying. Was spying always bad? Isla had spied on Mum, getting into her computer and reading that letter, which meant they could start their mission. She slid the ring off her middle finger and used its sharp corner to dig into another itchy place on her arm, and pushed it back onto her thumb, where it was tighter. She rubbed its patterns against her lips and kissed it.

Mum, where are you? Isla mouthed up to the clouds. Hermione Granger wouldn't be feeling pathetic like this, thought Isla. She'd devise a clever plan to find Mum AND foil a plot by rival wizards. And have loads of fun with Harry and Ron along the way. But all she had was Lac and Weasley. Let's face it, a little kid and a hamster weren't ideal partners. She needed wizards.

The clouds were no longer pink but a dirty yellow, forming weird shapes like mountains in the sky. *Mum, what made you come here?* The words repeated in her head, until she was too cold to sit any longer. It still wasn't quite dark. She stood up and walked about, stretching her stiff legs. Everything felt unreal, as if she'd stepped into a movie.

She unzipped the tent to check on Lac. Weasley had curled up inside one of his shoes. She backed out again with Luke Skywalker in her hand, and Isla held him in front of her. Luke looked at her with blue eyes while Isla scratched her neck. Another bite.

'What do you think? You're good at solving problems. Is our Mum still here?'

Isla sat Luke on the ground and slid her hands into warm pockets. Luke looked at her.

'We've followed Mum to this island. But now what? How are we going to track her footsteps if we don't know where she went?'

That stone-like feeling returned to her stomach. Isla felt stupid. How could two kids travel hundreds of miles across the sea to look for their Mum, who was – *say it, Isla.* Who was – missing? Like that advert on a billboard at home. *Have you seen so-and-so?* And a picture of an ordinary-looking person. *Missing since such-and-such a date.* How long had Mum been – Isla hesitated – missing? But how would that help? *It's not when she went that matters, it's where she is now.*

Isla shivered in the half-dark. She picked Luke up again and stared him in the face. She wished she hadn't eaten the whole of her chocolate bar.

'Are you telling me that there's only us? No-one else is going to look for Mum, so we've got to look for clues and work it out somehow? Thanks a lot.'

What clues? There wouldn't be a poster stuck in the road saying, 'Mum this way,' with an arrow pointing which way to go. Astronauts have Plan A and then Plan B in case the first plan goes wrong. But Isla only had one plan; there was no Plan B.

In the dim light, she brushed her teeth while the wind whistled. Beyond the rocks, huge waves thundered up the beach. Giant rollers crashed over rocks, one after another, as if they wanted to smash everything in their path and drag weaklings into the sea's depths.

Leaving her trainers next to Lac's outside the tent, Isla unzipped the door and wriggled inside, pulled the brush through her knotty hair and put her zinger in her pocket. Shivering, she slipped inside her sleeping bag, and lay next to her brother's warm body but couldn't stop shaking and thinking about the scary rough sea just a few metres away, and Lac nearly drowning.

A horrible thought circled in her mind: *Mum can't swim.*

CHAPTER 15

KIDNAPPER

Isla woke up desperate for a pee. Lac's eyes were open. His fingers were making shapes and swooping, chasing the shadows in the tent. She pulled herself out of the sleeping bag and found Weasley snuffling in the pile of clothes by their feet. As soon as she unzipped the tent, Weasley hopped outside and started to nibble grass and clover. Isla laid a handful of grass inside his nest and placed him on top of it. Wriggling into her jeans, she put on her zinger, told Lac where she was going, and scrambled behind a rock.

As she squatted, Isla watched a flock of long-legged seabirds skittering on the shore, sticking their sharp red beaks into the barren sand, squeaking with each step. She tried counting them, but they kept moving. There were at least seventeen. So what? How was counting birds going to help find Mum? She pulled up her jeans. Maybe they should have gone the other way to the visitor centre and asked the adults for help. But would they help? She scraped her fingers through her hair. Isla was afraid that she and Lac would be taken away and no-one would bother to find Mum. She couldn't take the risk – better for her and Lac to look for Mum on their own.

When Isla came back, the second milk bottle lay upended – empty – next to Lac, sitting in his pants alongside a crumpled chocolate biscuit wrapper. He was gorging a packet of crisps that he must have found somewhere in their stash.

'Don't just throw your crisp packet.' Isla caught it as it blew past her and stuffed it in her pocket. She paused for a moment. 'Hang on. Where'd you find those crisps?'

Lac gave a sideways smile.

'You hid them?' Isla pulled the empty pink packet from her pocket. 'But we didn't buy any Prawn Cocktail.'

That silly smile was still on his face.

'You stole them? From the shop? And that chocolate biscuit?'

The smile broadened, and he put his hands on his hips, elbows sticking out, as if to say: *So there!*

'You little robber. Did you nick anything else?'

The smile faded. He pulled on his trackie bottoms and trainers, ran over barnacle-covered rocks and jumped down to the beach.

'Hey! Come back!' But he was gone.

Up in the sky, a seagull spread wide its white wings, its black head bobbing downward.

'Squew-ew, squew-ew!'

On the beach below, Lac replied, 'Squew-ew, squew-ew!' holding his arms out like wings and trotting great semi-circles on the hard sand. The scrape on his face looked raw.

Isla humphed and rooted in his bag but there was nothing to eat. No food left in her rucksack, either. She mixed a sachet of Nesquik with water – not exactly tasty, but it filled the empty space in her stomach.

A slight movement caught Isla's eye. A brown and orange butterfly landed on a large pebble and opened its wings, its antennae waving. Tiptoeing nearer to the delicate creature, Isla saw its orange-splodged wings, bordered by black lines, until a gust of wind swept the butterfly into the air. Up and away, out of reach and soon out of sight, way before it reached the seagull which was still gliding in huge arcs high in the sky.

'*Craark!!*' A huge brown bird dive-bombed the gull. It darted away just in time. '*Squew-ew, squew-ew.*'

The brown bird copied the gull's spiral flight, squawking *'craark! craark!'* from its curved beak and closed in on its prey, chasing it higher and higher, until the gull escaped, and the brown bird peeled away and returned to its spot over the shore.

Isla pulled a sock over her toes.

'Hey!' came a shout. 'Where's your sister?'

She spun her head round. A tall man in a black hoody was bending down and putting his arm round Lac's shoulders.

'No!!' she screamed, and launched herself over the rocks, scraping her hands and bare foot on the sharp barnacles. She raced along the beach and leapt on the man's back. 'You're not taking him!'

The man staggered and fell to the sand with Isla on top of him.

'Leg it, Lac!' Isla yelled, while she punched and kicked every bit of the body beneath her that her fists and knees and feet could find.

'Ooofff! Umphh!' cried the kidnapper.

Isla kept up the battering, her hair flying as she swung her fists and shouted. From the corner of her eye she spotted Lac belting along the beach. She yanked a fistful of long sandy-red hair.

'You're not getting us.'

Every second gave Lac a chance to get away.

'*Squew-ew.*' Up in the sky, reinforcements had arrived. The single white bird had become a crowd of gulls above them, calling as if they were cheering a fight in the playground at school. The brown bird darted and retreated several times, looking for the weakest one to attack.

'Get off, you bampot, it's me,' breathed the kidnapper in a split-second pause while Isla gasped for breath.

He arched his back and Isla fell onto the sand. She curled up into a ball, arms protecting her head, ready for a beating.

'Yer great numpty,' the man said.

Isla opened her eyes. 'You?' It was Archie, the boy from the shop.

'And a fine welcome you've given me,' he replied. 'Don't you have manners where you come from?' *Yoo* again.

Isla ignored his outstretched hand. Sweat stung her eyes and she rubbed them to try and see more clearly.

'I saw you from my tractor. I've come to help you,' he said, 'as you're still looking for your ma – '

'How do you know? Have you been spying on us?' She stood up and screwed her eyes half-closed against the bright light as she looked up at him. He shrugged.

'You wouldn't be out here if you'd found her.' He bent over and sand sprinkled towards his feet as he raked bony fingers through his hair. Isla couldn't see his face.

'Do you want my help?' he asked.

Isla looked down, digging circles in the sand with her big toes. He was older than her and sounded like he was telling the truth. Could she trust him, or was he fooling about like most boys?

'How do I know you're not messing?'

He flicked his hair back and looked down at her. 'Just believe me, honest.'

'We don't have any choice,' mumbled Isla.

Something wasn't right. 'Hang on – what do you know about our Mum?'

'There was someone who talked like you in the shop this week. A woman, so it was.'

Did he mean Mum? Isla felt a squeeze in her chest.

'She's alive? This isn't a joke, is it?' Isla couldn't look him in the eye. 'What do you mean, talked like us. Talked like what?'

'You know, like you say "dye" when you mean "day".'

She felt sick. Her heart hammered in her chest as if it was trying to break out of prison.

'What're you talking about?' she asked, clenching her stomach to try and stop the hiccups that were threatening to start.

'I've got a Scottish accent, yeah?'

'Yeah.'

'An' you've got a –, you talk like –' He spread out his arms, searching for the word.

'Brummie.'

He clicked his fingers. 'Yeah, that's it. Not many of your lot around here. One came to the shop.'

'When?' Isla whispered, her trembling fingers twisting a strand of hair round and round.

'Day before you came. She bought a few messages and walked away down this road,' he replied in a matter-of-fact tone.

'Messages?' This boy was dense. No-one goes into a shop for messages, and anyway you don't *buy* messages. Unless it was different on this island.

'That's right.'

'Phone messages?' It still didn't compute.

'No, milk and bread and stuff,' he replied.

'Oh, shopping, you mean.' Isla paused. She looked towards the strip of tarmac. 'That road?'

'There's only the one road on this side of the island.'

A clue at last. Thoughts raced through Isla's head. She imagined Mum's surprised face when they turned up, followed by a broad grin and huge hug. Everything would be okay again. She'd tell them why she came to the island.

Isla opened her mouth to thank the boy, but a shriek came out instead. 'Lac! Where's Lac?' She looked along the empty beach stretching into the distance. She felt cold all over.

'We've got to find Lac.'

CHAPTER 16

STINGS

Isla narrowed her eyes against sharp grains of sand blowing into her face.

'He ran that way,' she shouted.

They looked in the direction Lac had fled. Not a single person on the beach, but in the sea two adults and a child were splashing in the shallows, jumping over breaking waves and laughing, all holding hands.

'We've lost him, thanks to *you,*' Isla said, sounding like *yow.*

'Because of you,' the boy said, sounding like *yoo.* 'We'll find him, right enough.'

Twisting round on her heel, Isla ran up to the road, where the boy had left his tractor. The sun scudded out from behind banks of cloud and slid back in again. In a field, a dog jumped off the back of a farmer's quad bike and skipped around the sheep, barking, herding them towards a gate. No small boy in sight.

She rushed back to the beach. The sea was racing to the shore, crashing its foaming breakers and retreating with a roar. She and the boy ran along the beach calling out, 'Lac. La-a-a-ac!'

Something stabbed her foot. 'Owwwww!' Isla hopped and looked back at a mass of pink fronds splayed on the beach.

'That frickin' jellyfish got me.'

'Let's have a look.' The boy prodded the sole of her foot, while Isla steadied herself with her hand on his shoulder.

'Not too bad, there's no stinging spines stuck in your skin.'

'Ow! Stop poking!'

'You need to bathe it in seawater.'

'Can't. Got to find Lac.'

A flame of pain shot through her foot when it touched the sand, and Isla limped along the beach, shouting for Lac.

'Lac, come out. It's ok.' Isla strained her ears. Was that a small noise mixed with the wind? She couldn't be sure.

'Mew, mew.'

Archie's long legs caught up with her.

'Listen,' she said.

'Mew, mew, mew.'

'Don't be afraid,' she called. 'It's only that boy, Archie.'

'"*Only* Archie" – thanks a bunch.' He clenched his fists.

The bird call floated through the air again. 'Mew, mew.'

'This way,' called Archie.

They ran up the beach away from the sea, and found Lac huddled into a hollow in a sandy bank.

'It's a wee lamb's hideout,' Archie laughed.

'Don't be mean,' Isla said, gathering her shuddering brother into her arms, kneeling to pull him closer. 'The boy didn't come to capture us,' she told him.

'Mew,' Lac said. As Isla felt his body relax and soften, he uttered a quiet 'cheepy-cheep.' Isla ruffled his ginger hair. Archie joined in.

'You're a bonnie boy aren't you? Watch out for your hair though – your sister ripped a whole chunk of mine.' He rubbed his head and grinned. 'She's dangerous.'

Bonnie boy. That phrase scratched at the back of Isla's brain.

As soon as they'd calmed down, Isla realised the pain in her foot was agony.

'It feels like it's on fire.'

'Come here,' Archie said, helping her to stand and pulling her arm up and round his shoulder so that Isla was slightly lifted off her feet. Lac jumped up and reached to pull her free.

'C'mon, wee 'un, we need to get your sister down to the sea. She's stood on a jellyfish.'

'Skreek!'

'What?'

White spots flashed in her eyes. Supported by Archie, Isla hopped towards the waves. They splashed straight in, up to their ankles. When she lowered her foot, the shock of cold water made her cry out.

'Ow-oh!' Relief, as the cold soothed her throbbing foot. 'Oooh, it's heaven.' But after a moment the pain returned.

'It's stinging again, ow-ow!'

'The salt will be helping.'

'I knew that already.'

'Okay, okay,' Archie muttered under his breath. 'You're a hard one to please.'

Her mind flashed back to history lessons, Nelson's sailors screaming as salt was packed into their cannonball wounds. School belonged to a different world. Isla felt like she'd swapped lives with another Isla and become a new person - the sort of girl who lives in the wild, where seawater heals wounds. Kayla, Aunty Lou, Miss Henry, trumpet lessons, all felt unreal, like a dream. This mission was her real life.

The waves washed round their legs. Isla stood squashed in the middle between two red-haired lads, one big and one little. The fiery ball of the sun hung in the sky, giving the sea a silvery glitter. Everything was blurred. Isla closed her eyes and drew in a deep breath.

'Any better?' Archie asked.

'Pardon?' The crashing waves had blotted out his words. 'You're on my wrong side. My zinger doesn't always catch what people are saying.' Isla held her hand above her eyes and looked up at him against the bright white clouds. He was much taller than her.

'Are you feeling better?' he shouted.

'Yes.' Isla breathed out. 'Yes, quite a bit. But my eyes aren't working properly. And don't shout.'

Still holding Archie's arm, Isla hobbled out of the sea, with Lac steering her elbow, and flopped onto the sand.

'Thanks.' Isla rubbed her eyes and a lump in her throat turned into tears. 'Your boots are soaking,' Isla said.

'Oh well, worse things have happened.' He sat down, unlaced them and pulled them off, and tugged at his socks. A stream of water dripped onto the sand as he squeezed them with fierce twists.

Letting the tears dry on her cheeks, Isla realised she could see properly again.

'I've been looking for you,' Archie said, not shouting.

'We're okay, we're fine, leave us alone.'

'Oh yeah? Like that's really true?' he laughed.

'We don't need any help.' Isla sat up straighter, sticking her chin out.

'No? Look at you. Your jeans are muddy, you clearly slept in your clothes, your hair's all over the place.'

Isla tried to rake her fingers through her hair. 'I brushed it yesterday. Day before.' Why couldn't she remember? She always brushed her hair. Loads of times every day. But now Isla didn't even know where her hairbrush was.

'And look at the wee one's poor face.'

'He fell over.' She got up. 'C'mon Lac, jump on my back, we're off.' Spreading her arms wide, Lac sprang up behind her and fixed his arms round her neck.

Isla walked a few paces on her aching foot.

Behind her, Archie mumbled something.

'What was that?' Isla stopped and turned. She couldn't see his face. He was just an outline against the glare of the sun.

Even though she didn't believe in magic, Isla wished right then that Hermione Granger would appear on the beach, flick her wand, and apparate them to wherever Mum was.

'Nothing,' he said. He stuck his hands in the pockets of his cargo pants.

Isla couldn't think properly. The noise of the surf in her ears, pain still shooting up her body from her foot, the blinding sun.

'Do you want me to help you find your Ma or not?'

Isla said nothing. Lac leant heavily on her back.

'She doesnae know you're here, does she?'

Isla shook her head and bit her tongue to stop tears filling her eyes.

Lac couldn't keep quiet. 'Skreek, skreek, skreek,' he trilled. 'Irripp, irripp-pip,' and slid off Isla's back.

'What's up with him?'

'He's saying: Have you really seen our Mum?'

Archie gave Lac a sideways look and shrugged his shoulders.

Without waiting for an answer, he walked back along the beach and up past the rocks to their tent. Isla and Lac followed, hand in hand. Isla felt numb, wordless. If she had her trumpet, its notes could sing her feelings. But she'd left it behind, and anyway it wasn't even hers, it belonged to school, so she had to live without it.

With Archie's help, they bundled up the tent and packed up their rucksacks. Archie made encouraging noises – 'There now,' and 'Nearly done,' as he tightened the straps on Isla's pack, and 'Grand' while he hoisted Lac's bag easily over his shoulder. Lugging her stuff, Isla limped along the road. Lac trotted next to Archie, carrying Weasley's nest bag under his arm and uttering high-pitched trills.

'Hop on the tractor and I'll take you along the way.' He kept brushing his long ginger hair away from where it fell over his eyes. Something about the way he spoke made her feel like she'd met him before. Not just him. Everything felt kind of familiar, as if she'd had another life before this one, like Manpreet at school and his family believed. Maybe this was what they meant.

They climbed up onto the dirty plastic seat, which was shaped for a bigger person, and the edge cut into their thighs. As the boy swung into his seat behind the wheel, he spat several times.

'Yeuch! The midgies are bad today.'

'The what?'

'Midgies. Looks like they've been eating you to death, and all.'

'Oh, them.' She rubbed her face and neck. 'Have you got any food?' Isla asked.

'What?'

He started the engine, and its loud throb matched the din in her ears.

'Mewwwww,' went Lac.

'What's he saying?' shouted the boy above the noise of the engine.

'He's hungry,' Isla yelled back. 'Have you got anything to eat?'

'Oh. No.'

The tractor jumped as he pushed the gear stick. 'Wait, I've got this.' He leaned back and pulled a pack of Juicy Fruit chewing gum from his pocket.

'We'll have it.' Isla held out her hand. 'Thanks,' remembering her manners while tearing at the yellow wrapper and silver foil and shoving a stick into her mouth. Out of the corner of her eye she could see Lac doing the same.

The boy bounced in his seat. 'Funny,' he said. 'It's like Home Alone in reverse.'

With a jolt, the tractor moved off the grass verge and started to roll along the road.

'Hold on,' Archie shouted, 'don't want to lose you, do I?' He laughed and the engine went *Vroom!* as he pressed his foot on the accelerator. 'The midgies will never keep up with us.'

Isla wanted to scream. How could he laugh when they were so desperate?

The tractor's engine hummed *Find Mum, Find Mum, Find Mum.*

Archie looked behind at two lines of wild flowers squashed by gigantic tyre tracks. 'Oops, bit of damage to the machair there.'

Bump, bump, bump. That was Isla's heart, not the tractor. Something wasn't right. The boy kept looking across at her and Lac and grinning.

'What?'

'Nothing.' There was only room for one car on the narrow road. He focused his eyes on the two lines of tarmac either side of tufts of grass sprouting out of the middle.

'You know *Home Alone*?'

'Yes.'

'You're like those kids, except you're not at home.' He screwed his eyes up against the sun in his face, and chuckled.

Isla didn't like his laugh. 'It's not funny.'

He was still smirking. 'No, of course not.' He looked at her again, and a farty noise came out of his nostrils.

This wasn't fair. He was supposed to be helping them, but instead he was laughing at them.

'Stop. I want to get out.'

'Huh? D'you want to relieve yourself?'

What was he talking about?

'This'll do. We'll carry on from here. You're sure she went this way? Along this road?'

'If you say so. Like I said, there's only the one road.' He braked and yanked up the handbrake. 'This is so random. Are you sure now?'

'Yes, we'll keep going and –' Isla couldn't finish the sentence.

'Peep-peep,' went Lac.

'Awful friendly, aren't we?' he shouted over his shoulder as the engine throbbed back into life.

Standing at the roadside, they watched the tractor turn in a large circle and re-join the road, leaving tyre tracks in the wild-flowery land. 'And thanks,' Isla shouted, 'we have got manners in Brum.' What a cheek!

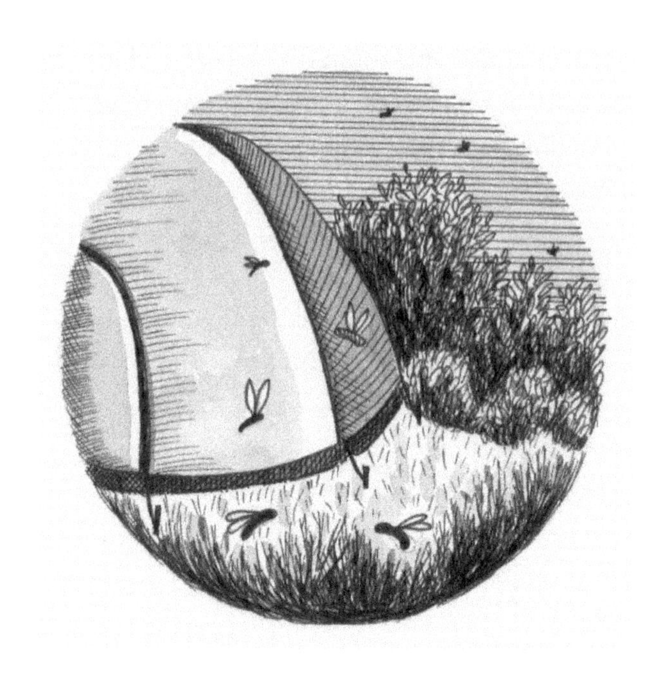

CHAPTER 17

ENDLESS ROAD

They sat on the grass verge, sweltering. Isla closed one eye and squinted up to the sky. The dazzling white sun made everything shimmer. *Mum, I need Mum, she's got to be somewhere.* She still had no idea what made Mum come here.

Lac jumped up and slapped at his legs. He darted about, flapping his arms and squeaking like the red-beaked birds on the beach. Isla felt something creeping on her ankle.

'Ergghh, ree-volting! There's millions of them.'

Above their heads, skreeking gulls were snapping their beaks at a black cloud of insects filling the sky. A carpet of winged ants crawled around Isla and Lac's feet and crept up their legs. Smacking their trousers, they leapt from foot to foot trying to dodge the flying army swarming around their heads, as if they were practising for a break-dancing competition with added squeaks and whoops. But their shrieks did not sound like fun.

They fled along the road, heads down, their feet pounding on the tarmac, until the cloud of ants thinned and finally disappeared. Isla felt better by themselves. There was something about that boy that made her feel strange. Scary but also – he was acting superior, as if he knew things that she didn't, but wouldn't say. They were better off without him.

Isla's foot was still hurting, but they plodded on, one foot after another. Looking sideways beyond the road's grassy verge, Isla wondered about the long wild grass speckled with pink, yellow and blue flowers that stretched towards a mountain. Was this 'machair'?

Now they were clear of the ants, Isla's hunger pains started up again. Lac strutted along, head poking upwards, and his song rang out clearly. 'Chirrup-irrup-ruppity-rup,' he sang. He sounded happy, as if he had found a new home. Strange, since earlier today he was a total misery-guts. And they were still starving and lost and might be – Isla juddered – orphans.

Those swirly patterns on Mum's ring had to be a clue. It definitely held some sort of link with the island. Her fingertips felt for the familiar cross, but the ring wasn't on her thumb. She remembered taking it off in the dark last night and holding it against her heart. She scrabbled in her pocket but it wasn't there.

Handing Weasley's carrier over to Lac, Isla threw her pack to the hard ground, pulled everything out, and shoved her hand into its empty space. Nothing. She shook it upside down and a pile of stuff clattered out of the side pockets. But no ring. Blinking away sweat dribbling into her eyes, she felt into every corner. Lac traced a pattern on a patch of dirt with the toe of his shoe.

'I've lost Mum's ring! I need it,' she sobbed.

Lac rummaged in the jumbled tent, his beady eyes darting back and forth. Something glinted. But it was only a metal peg dangling from a guy rope in his hand.

'I can't believe it's lost,' she hiccupped, shoving everything back in her pack. She stood up and glugged some water from her bottle. She rubbed her stomach to try and stop it hurting 'We need food.'

'Wirry-irri-up?' Lac danced around but Isla couldn't work out what he was saying.

'I don't know.' Her hand over her forehead like she'd seen Mum do, Isla sheltered her eyes from the sun and looked down the bare road. 'Maybe there's a shop along here.' *Shop = food.*

Lac handed Weasley back to her, and they set off once more. They trudged for ages, but there was no shop. *Keep going.* Things didn't always work out for Hermione, but that didn't stop her trying.

At last, the sun drifted down towards the horizon and it wasn't so hot.

Lac disappeared behind some yellow-flowered bushes. He was squatting on a patch of grass hidden from the road. 'Craaark'. He patted the ground and rabbit-hopped around the enclosure. Isla took the hint, off-loaded her rucksack and they both yanked at her pack, untangling the tent between them.

'Peepity-peep-peep,' Lac clucked as he bustled about pushing pegs into the soft ground while Isla fitted the poles together. It seemed like Lac had that same familiar feeling. It was as if he already knew these birds before he got here. He wiggled inside and stood holding the tent above his head, making it easy for Isla to slot the poles into their grommets.

'Wow, you've really got the hang of this.'

Lac looked just like a bird preening its feathers, all fluffed up and proud. He shoved their sleeping bags into place and lay down. Isla stood and looked above the bush that was hiding them. On the other side of the road, a rotting wooden boat lay on the beach, half-sunk in the sand, with grass and flowers growing on its leaning deck. Behind the tent, a stretch of flowery machair gave way to fields, and in the distance scrubby ground rose steeply up the side of a mountain.

The sun floated low over the sea and slowly sank out of sight. Isla peered into the half-dark, where hazy white, orange and green shapes hovered like spaceships. As her eyes adjusted, the mystery mounds transformed into a bunch of tents spread out across a field. She clenched her fists. Tents meant people. People equalled danger but they might also mean help.

'What do you think, Ron Weasley?' Isla hardly ever called him by his full name, but things were getting serious. She'd got away with pretending to be sixteen on the train, but Weasley agreed it wouldn't work again. His snout quivering in her cupped hands reminded her of a fox scavenging at night around the wheelie bins on their street.

Scavenging – that was an idea. She sniffed. A smell of frying floated in the air, and her tongue watered as pictures of sausages and bacon and fried bread swam in front of her eyes. Weasley sucked on her little finger, and Isla knew she had to make a decision. Whatever she did, she couldn't take Lac with her.

'Lac,' she called. He crawled out of the tent and strutted and bobbed his head forward and back like a pigeon. He got down on his hands and knees and started pecking the grass.

'Hungry?' Isla asked. 'I've worked out another task on our mission.' Beaky nodding and little hops. 'I gonna find some food. You've got to stay here and be lookout.'

Lac dived back inside the tent and emerged again holding Luke Skywalker.

Isla pointed to the field which was still visible. Looked like it was never going to get properly dark. If she didn't mention the bunch of hairy caramel-coloured cows she had to pass before getting there, maybe they wouldn't be so scary.

'I'm going to scout out that campsite.'

He furrowed his eyebrows and hopped around her in rapid circles. Every time Isla tried to walk away, he jumped in front of her. Then he pushed his head into her body and held on round her waist.

'Don't panic,' Isla said. 'Here, look after Weasley while I'm gone.' At the touch of the warm fur on his neck, Lac released his hold, shoved Luke in his waistband and took Weasley in both hands.

'I'll be back soon. Lookout is an important job. You're doing sentry duty, like Finn watching out for Kylo Rey. Make sure our stuff is safe. But if anyone comes past, make sure you hide. And if you're in danger, make a noise.'

'Craaaarkk.'

'Perfect.'

CHAPTER 18

NEWS AT NIGHT

A soreness like prickly needles spread across Isla's foot as she sprinted across the machair to the field. Close up, the cows' long horns looked really sharp. Could she get past without disturbing them? The hunger pains in her stomach made her brave. She wriggled under the fence, ran sideways along a fence, and jumped a ditch at the other end.

Lights shone from a gleaming white caravan at the edge of the site. Isla gasped when she heard a television voice murmuring through its open window. *Haven't seen any TV for ages.* But her excitement didn't last – it was only the news. *Boring!* Bent low, she used the caravan's side as cover to scan the rest of the site before the next stage of her mini-mission. The muffled television commentary calmed her down and Isla's heartbeats slowed as sweat dripped off her forehead.

She was about to move away when she heard the words '……..fake campaigners…'

That word *fake* again. As in not real. As in pretend. Greta Thunberg is a campaigner. Does campaign mean the same as protest?

Isla pictured Mum and Dad, a load of other people, masses of tents. Kids playing with guns made of wire that the adults had cut from a fence. *Where did that thought come from?*

Had Isla heard right? She tilted her head upwards towards the opening to give her good ear its best chance.

The man's voice continued, '…..police officers were deployed…..'

Something pinged in her brain. She hugged her arms around herself. Why was she shivering?

The voice droned on. '…intimate relationships…..' Isla wasn't quite sure if that meant friends or more than that, with kissing and, you know, other stuff.

Isla leant against the caravan. That uneasy feeling resurfaced that Mum might be running away from trouble. She zoned back in on the voice, but he had moved on to announcing the weather forecast.

A dim glow from the back of a large square-framed tent a few metres away showed shapes inside. Shaking herself into "alert" mode, Isla crept closer, hearing murmurs and a lullaby tune that she vaguely recognised. At the side of the tent a pile of dirty dishes sat next to a half-covered pan. A not-empty frying pan.

Isla whispered Hermione's summoning charm. 'Accio!'

The lid made a tinny "tink" when Isla lifted it as slowly as she could. Holding her breath till she felt like she was going to burst, a baby voice said, 'More,' from inside the tent, and the singing started up again. *Day is done, Gone the sun, from the lake, from the hills, from the sky. All is well, safely rest……*

Three sausages, a brown crusty triangle, and something round and black landed in her pocket with one scoop. Isla nearly yelped with joy, but stopped herself, and skipped to the next pitch. Nothing. And the next. Two bread crusts in a plastic bag. Outside the sixth tent a promising plastic bag turned out to be rubbish. Rustling around inside it, Isla froze when a voice from inside said,

'What's that noise? Didn't you put the bag in the litter bin?'

Pulling a half-eaten burger from the mess of empty milk bottles, banana skins, food wrappings and dirty tissues, Isla scarpered. She hadn't needed Hermione's wand or bluebell flames. Just her own detective skills. Pockets bulging with scavenged stash, she jumped back over the ditch, slinked through the field past the scary cows, and raced across the machair into the gathering night.

After the stillness of the day, dark clouds were sweeping across the sky, and the moon popped out every now and then. Through a murky haze the horizon was no longer visible. Away from the quiet of the campsite, where she had been protected from the wind's growing fury, Isla became aware of the sound of sea crashing onto rocks.

Lac was as good as his word, standing watch over the tent. He saluted Isla. His eagle eyes spotted the sign of nosh poking out of her pockets, and he dived towards her.

'Here we go.' Isla emptied the mouth-watering pile onto the grass. 'Sausages…' But Lac already had his teeth round the burger and held the hash brown in his other hand.

'I guess I'll have the sausages,' Isla said, grinning. Forgetting for a moment what she had heard through the caravan window, she tucked in as if it was a full roast dinner.

We're going to find Mum, don't care what anyone says, even if she's in trouble. No-one had actually said they couldn't search for Mum, but they would if they knew about her and Lac's mission. She had to prove them wrong.

That night, howling wind and sheets of rain tugged at the tent, but Isla and Lac were warm and dry in their sleeping bags, while Weasley was curled up in his favourite shoe. Full of food, they dropped off to sleep.

CHAPTER 19

STORM

'Gerroff! Get off me!'

Warm breath blew on Isla's face. Her arms were trapped in the sleeping bag. Whirling wind rocked the tent. She bucked her body as hard as she could. She had to get free from the attacker. She curled like the Loch Ness monster and whumped upwards with a ferocious fling.

Thud! A whimper. *Torch, torch, torch*, thought Isla, as if saying the word would magic up the thing she'd forgotten to pack. Sitting up, she waved her arms in front and around her, as if she was swimming in the dark. The breaststroke movements brushed the top of Lac's head.

'Did he jump on you too?' she whispered.

Lac snivelled and tugged her t-shirt.

'Hang on.' Isla crawled to the front of the tent and felt around in the dark. 'All zipped up. Mystery.'

CRASH! A clap of thunder exploded above them. Isla ducked, and a white flash of lightning lit the tent for a milli-second. Lac jumped on her back, his whole body shaking, and he clapped his hands over his ears.

'Wha–? Was it you?'

Isla unclasped his legs and fumbled for her zinger. Fixing it in place, she heard a ghostly moan. A long, low, non-stop groan amidst the pelting rain and roar of the wind.

A distant rumbling joined the moaning, and a sharp glob of sick erupted into her mouth. Isla swallowed hard. She shuddered at the thought of phantoms flying around outside. *Don't think about the undead.* Ghosts don't exist. Not at home anyway. But here? She gulped, tried to take a deep breath but couldn't get it right down. Was it only the wind that was trying to tear the tent apart?

They clutched each other, and both jumped and screamed as a massive bang crashed over their heads, followed by a horrific ripping sound. Rain poured through a giant hole in the tent. Instantly, they were drenched.

Maybe an ogre had stamped out of the sea, swatting ghouls aside, who lay wounded and wailing, while the monster – .

'Run!'

Isla grabbed Lac's hand and pulled him through the gap in the side of the tent. In the wild darkness, barefoot on sodden grass, a mass of white shapes shimmered. Isla threw herself onto the ground.

Baaa-aa-aa, one of them said.

Back on their feet, Lac stumbled after Isla through a sheet of raindrops over the road to the beach. Isla hoisted him over the side of the abandoned fishing boat and belly-flopped onto the deck beside him.

'Crawl in there,' she told him, pointing to a gaping space where a door used to be.

He hesitated. Thunder crashed above them, filling the sky.

'Alright, I'll go first,' Isla shrieked, 'grab my ankle.'

Petrified, Isla dived head-first through the gap, and crawled into the dark cavern of the sand-filled wreck. Cold sand on her palms made her mouth go dry and her chest wheezed. Lac crept in behind her. It was a cabin, half full of sand – and dry.

Something pricked her knee.

Isla jerked away, hitting her head against the wooden wall, and felt hiccups surging up her throat. Working to calm her breath, she muttered,

'I am a hundred times bigger than a crab.'

She shivered as a faint picture formed behind her eyes. A big red pincer and a voice. *It'll nip you if you're naughty.* Dad. A tattoo on his arm. A massive red crab. The shiver ran up her back, and Isla shook it away.

Hic-hic-hiccup.

It felt like twenty crabs were swarming over her legs. Isla dared to put her hand down flat, ready to snatch it back before a crab nipped her. A tiny prick made her yank back.

'Hic.'

Holding her breath, Isla stuck out her forefinger and lowered it. Heartbeat pounding, body jiggling at each hiccup, Isla touched something hard and spiky. It didn't bite. It wasn't moving. She ran another finger along the thing's twig-like surface and picked it up. Definitely dead. Not even an animal.

'Hic.'

It was a piece of shrivelled seaweed that snapped when she squeezed it in her hand.

Isla let out her breath and her head flopped forward. Lac shuffled over on his bum, and they sat back to back, knees up, shivering, listening to the din of wind and rain. Chin on her knees, Isla tried to stop shaking. The hiccups subsided. She thought of Hermione being brave but also clever when she looked at the Basilisk through a mirror so she wouldn't be killed by its eyes locking onto hers.

'In the olden days, people thought a storm was the gods fighting each other and emptying water from the heavens. But we know it's just a storm, nothing to do with gods or ghosts. Don't we?'

Isla felt Lac nodding behind her.

'Enough about ghosts,' Isla said. 'Don't even say the word.'

She sucked a chunk of her hair. 'Except I just did.'

CHAPTER 20

EVERYTHING IS DIFFERENT

Something was different.

Isla rubbed her eyes in the daylight and uncurled her body. Silence. Stretching her cramped arms and legs, one by one, her muscles screamed with pain. Lac's eyes were open, and Isla burrowed back towards his warmth. Last night's escape flickered on replay behind her eyes.

'We survived.'

Isla lay on her aching shoulder and grinned. Lac beamed back.

'Your poor cheek,' Isla said, gently touching the graze. He pulled a face.

'Sorry.'

He touched her ear.

'Oops, forgot to take out my zinger.'

In the stillness Isla heard buzzing insects, the in-and-out of gentle surf and the rumble of sea breaking on rocks. Her reflection in his eyeballs was smiling but a moment later they mirrored her face in a panic.

'Where's Weasley?'

They crawled through the half-buried door of the cabin, the bright sunlight blinding them. Everything looked the same as yesterday morning. Waves rolling lazily onto the beach and retreating, seagulls strutting, burying their beaks in bundles of seaweed. Outlined against the sea, a row of birds stood to attention along the rocks. She could just see the top of a van moving along the road.

A vague image surfaced. A memory of sitting up high, seeing far ahead along the road from a vantage point in the front seat of a van. Seatbelt strapped around Mum and Isla, SuperTed squeezed between her and Dad.

This morning's breeze still carried a bite that made her shrug down into her puffer jacket. Fatty blobs of cloud splodged the blue-grey sky, looking innocent, unlike the previous evening's menacing clouds that had been the cause of last night's terror. Out at sea a fishing boat ploughed up and down through heavy waves. *I hope Mum wasn't out there in the storm,* Isla thought. She shook her shoulders and told herself to stop being ridiculous.

In the fields, sheep chomped grass. Behind the yellow-flowered spiky bushes, a bedraggled heap of tangled material and ropes lay in the place where their shiny blue tent had nestled in its grassy hiding place. Isla ran over and stood at the spot they'd briefly called home. The wind tangled her hair and rushed past her ears.

'The tent! Our things!' Isla pulled the stringy ends of her hair. 'Weasley!'

Lac got there first. 'Mew-ew-ew-ew.' He flitted around the ruined campsite.

Isla dropped onto her hands and knees. 'Weasley, where are you? You can come out, it's safe now.'

Lac got down on his front and squirmed like a worm under the sodden pile. Wriggling backwards, he emerged brandishing something in his hand: Luke Skywalker.

'Holy shapeshifter! Is that all you can think of?'

Isla gazed around the damp clearing. 'Where's Weasley? Where's all our stuff?' Isla kicked their spoiled belongings. There was no sign of Weasley amongst the crumpled material.

'What about our shoes?' She held up a broken pole that had split right down the middle.

'And where are we going to sleep?'

Isla kicked the mess again. Lac screwed up his eyes and pointed up the rise leading to the machair. A single trainer lay on its side.

He ran and picked it up, and uttered a new, excited noise. 'Piddip!' Trotting to a shallow ditch, he bent down. Another 'piddip!' Another shoe. But no Weasley. He darted around, collecting scattered items of their belongings, dumping them in front of their collapsed tent, and zooming off again to rescue more storm-blown stuff.

Isla sat down. The wet grass soaked her backside.

'We've got to find Weasley.'

She tipped out the remains of their food stash, which consisted of half a packet of mush that used to be bread.

'Not even Weasley's gonna want this,' she sobbed.

Next time Isla saw Lac walking back to their pitch, he had a glum face like Hermione's friend, Neville Longbottom, and was holding something dripping in front of him.

Oh no.

Then a flood of relief – it was only his iPad.

'Where was that?' she asked.

He pointed to a large puddle behind their ruined tent.

'Can you switch it on?' Isla remembered how he'd casually chuck it aside at home when it was teatime. He pressed the button, but the screen stayed blank. It reminded her of –.

'OH NO!' Isla dived into the crumpled doorway, worming her way right inside so only her feet stuck out. Water soaked her elbows and knees. The puddle was spreading under the groundsheet. Shoving her hand under the sleeping bag, her fingers found nothing furry, just something hard and cold. She pulled out her soggy book and underneath, rescued her phone.

'Phew! At least I've found my phone.' Her relief didn't last long. When she looked at the screen, she cried, 'I can't see anything. It's all foggy.'

Isla sat back on her knees with the wet tent draped around her shoulders, holding down the 'power' button. Still totally clouded. Pressing the home button made no difference. She tapped the screen – nothing – clicked the ringer switch, tried the volume controls – nothing. Crawling backwards out of the tent, Isla waved the phone about in the open air. Still cloudy.

'Couldn't ring for help if we wanted to.'

Lac pulled the two halves of the sodden tent apart and rooted around in its folds. He emerged holding a little bundle.

'Thank goodness.' Isla's chest was heaving, and she couldn't speak. But Lac didn't pass the hamster to Isla when she held out her hands. Isla reached out to touch Weasley's still body.

'He's – not moving.' She stood back. 'He is. His whiskers twitched.' She bent in again and looked for several seconds. 'Or was that the wind?'

She shuddered. 'Give him to me. He's probably hibernating. He needs warming up.' Isla took her little precious and stroked his back. 'Wake up, Weasley-Beasley.' He wasn't shivering like he normally did. Isla nuzzled his neck with her nose, but he didn't sniff or nibble. 'Come on, Weasley,' Isla said, 'it's okay now. Wake up.' His eyes stayed closed. Isla rubbed his cold stiff body and blew into the caked fur.

Lac appeared and nudged his head under her elbow.

'He's not moving,' Isla said. Lac stroked the still body with his finger. Tears fell onto their hamster's wet fur.

'We must have crushed him.' Isla let out a huge sob. 'We killed him!'

She stood, frozen on the spot, unmoving like her little furry treasure. She couldn't think of any more words. Everything was going wrong. She sank down onto her knees, hands cradling Weasley. Lac sat next to her, and Isla leant into his messy hair. The two of them sat for a long time, shivering despite the warm sun.

Isla's stomach grumbled.

'We're on our own,' she said. 'We were alone before, but now we really are.' She stood up. 'Come on, we've got to do something.' *Can't sit here all day,* Mum would have said.

Lac slipped away, squawking and hopping like a bird with a broken leg. He pulled a woolly hat from the tent wreckage, flicked off some dirt, and held it out. Isla wrapped up Weasley's delicate body and put him in her pocket.

They pulled the rucksacks and sleeping bags from their muddied belongings and laid everything out to dry in the sun. Some hope. Spreading the remains of the tent on the grass, Isla saw it was well and truly wrecked, torn right across.

'That's the end of Scout Camp,' she said. As if that mattered. Nothing about home was important now.

'Ropes might come in useful,' she muttered, grunting as she tried to untie the knots attached to loops at each corner of the tent. Giving up, she shoved it all – tent and everything – into her still-wet rucksack with the single unbroken pole. Isla pushed herself up from the damp ground, her stained jeans dripping brown goo. She smeared tears out of her eyes and licked her salty lips. They had to find Mum.

She couldn't just be gone. She'd always been there, her troubled Mum. Mum the beautiful. Mum the brave. They couldn't give up now. They belonged together. Something had happened to make her leave. If only they could find her.

CHAPTER 21

FOOD

Fury bubbled in Isla's chest as they stood aside to let a builder's van, a few cars and several campervans pass by. *Can't they see we need help? We're starving?* Isla told herself to stop thinking like that. If a driver stopped to help, they would want to know what she and Lac were doing. They needed to keep well away from interfering adults. She forced herself to wave back at the drivers, as if they were on an innocent walk, not a desperate mission. Her fingers recoiled every time her hand went to her pocket where her fingertips encountered a wad of cold, wet wool enclosing her beloved Weasley.

The shop boy said Mum had gone this way. If only some sort of sign would tell them where she was.

Away from the beach, the road curved around a hill. The weather was strangely calm, but they had to fight through huge clouds of those pesky midges. It seemed like only the wind kept them away. A bunch of black-faced sheep munched outside a farm gate. Inside the gate, a rutted drive full of puddles disappeared as it curved uphill. Isla looked to right and left. There was no-one in sight, and no cars on the road as it re-joined the beach to run alongside another bay. A rocky headland jutted out to sea in the distance.

Isla waited. Still no cars or people.

'Ssshhh,' she whispered, finger on her lips. 'Wait here.'

She approached a box fixed to the wall marked 'Eggs. £1.50 per half dozen.' She opened the lid and plunged her hand inside, pulled out a box of eggs and slammed the lid, all in one movement.

'Come on.' She ran, Lac close behind her, scanning the beach for a hiding place. They found a secluded hollow. Sitting with their backs against warm rocks, two charred planks lay on top of a heap of grey ash.

'Looks like someone had a fire here, out of the wind.'

Careful to avoid rusty nails, Isla picked up a plank and touched the blackened end. Something hovered in her brain. She poked the ashes with her finger. They were warm. Maybe someone had cooked some food here last night.

Isla dumped her rucksack and opened the box to find six beautiful brown eggs.

'I'm so clever,' she sang, and rummaged in her bag for the spork. 'We just have to build a fire, and whizzbang! Scrambled eggs.' She'd learned how to do this at Scout Camp. Once the fire had died down, all you had to do was blow on the red-hot coals to get it going again. Isla puffed gently in the ashes, and a tiny red ember glowed. She blew again, and a cloud of ash flew up but there were no wisps of smoke. Lac threw his pack on the ground and gathered a few twigs of dried seaweed. Isla poked one into the ash and blew, but there was no spark. *Please, please, pleee-ase,* she murmured. A brighter speck flared for a moment, then went out.

'I'm so stupid.' Isla slapped her forehead. 'Dumb-brain! No lighter. Not even any matches.'

She picked at bits of rubbish that were caught in the rocks, praying that maybe, just maybe someone had dropped a lighter. If it still worked, they could get a fire going and break the eggs into –

'No frying pan.'

Isla sat down with a thunk, elbows on knees. There was no crying left in her. Lac sat beside her and leant his head on her knee. A seagull swooped above them with a fish poking out of its beak.

'Maybe we could catch a fish,' she said.

But she knew they couldn't, not really.

'How come you're allowed to catch fish?' she shouted to the seagull, which had deposited its treasure on a rock and was already fighting off marauders who wanted some of its booty.

'Anyway, we couldn't cook a fish,' she said.

They searched the beach, looking for ideas. Anything they could eat. Lac touched a see-through jellyfish with the toe of his trainer. It was like a floppy umbrella without any spines, pink circles lacing through its squidgy shape.

'Yuk, not that.'

The creature gave her the jitters even though Isla knew it was stranded. But when the tide carried it out to sea again, its long tentacles could sting you. *Stupidddd*, Ally said in her head. Isla was scared of something that hadn't even happened. But what if? What if you got stung in the sea? What if that had happened to Mum? What if she'd tripped like Lac in the pond and banged her head and no-one found her?

Isla took three deep breaths, like Mum had taught her. 'Chin up,' she'd say. Isla lifted her chin, shook her hair behind her back, and stepped away from the jellyfish. At the tideline, a crowd of gulls were bobbing their black heads into shallow water.

'It's so unfair. Those measly birds get to eat, but we don't,' she said.

They roamed among the rocks, but the pools disappointed them. No fish, just water and seaweed. Isla popped a slimy seaweed bubble and a milky liquid oozed out. She flinched at the dirty salty taste when she touched it with her tongue.

When they got back to their hiding place, the pain in her stomach was nibbling her insides like a mouse. Or a gnawing rat. Isla had to think of something. If only Hermione was real and came to help them. She'd had to put up with hate mail and screaming howlers, so a little problem like having food she couldn't cook would never beat her.

Isla opened the box of eggs and fumbled in her pack for the empty milk bottle. Holding it between her knees, she took an egg from the box, carefully cracked it with the spork and emptied the contents through the opening of the milk bottle. A bit of goo dribbled down the sides but most of it went in. She did this six times. She screwed on the lid and shook it hard. Inside, a yellow frothy liquid started to form. She shook it harder, roaring like an angry gorilla, so loud that Lac put his hands over his ears. It felt like her arm would drop off from so much shaking.

Unscrewing the lid, Isla took a deep breath, squeezed her eyes shut, raised the bottle to her mouth, tipped it up, and swallowed. *Ugh*. One. She did it again. *Yuk*. Two. And again. *Eurgh*. Three. This was like Hermione's disgusting Polyjuice Potion, but without any magic. She held her breath to stop hiccups jerking her body up and down.

Isla passed the bottle to Lac. He took a sip and pushed it away in disgust.

'Do it like this.' She took another big disgusting swallow. 'C'mon. The rest is for you. It's food.' She thrust the bottle into his hands.

Isla pulled at her lips and sucked her teeth to try and get rid of the slimy taste.

'It's space food. Like Luke Skywalker eats.' *Hic.*

He looked sideways at her as he brought it to his mouth.

'Honestly,' Isla said. *Hic.*

He tipped it up, gulped the whole lot down, threw the bottle away and started coughing. Isla bashed him on the back.

'Come on, warrior. Don't peg out.'

Lac burped and went, 'Krrr-krrr-krrr.'

Isla went, *Hic-hic-hic.*

Isla didn't really care anymore what happened to her, but she still had to look after Lac. Even though she felt so terrible, she still retrieved the bottle. No littering. Greta says always look after the environment: there's no Planet B.

CHAPTER 22

GOODBYE WEASLEY

Isla sat looking out to sea and feeling sick while the hiccups went away. Was that breakfast or dinner? And what about tea? She took off her shoes and socks. Her feet felt disgusting. Isla scraped grey globs from between her toes and tried to make herself feel better by imagining Ally eating those eggs and being sick.

Missing since whatever date. Isla pictured that poster she'd seen from the bus on the way to school. The photos were someone's brother or sister or mum looking at her through the bus window.

The bump-bump, bump-bump, bump-bump of her heart rocked the mass of congealed egg in her stomach. Chewing her tongue, she tried not to throw up.

If we find Mum, she'll make us garlic bread and pasta bake, sloppy with cheese. Isla looked back the way they'd come. *If? What do I mean, If? I mean When not If. We're not orphans. Not unless Mum has –.* Isla didn't like this conversation in her head. Mum was depressed sometimes, but she wasn't – well, she got better, and then things were okay again. Anyway, Mum's got her and Lac. *She hasn't. She's left us.* Isla swallowed the lump in her throat, which hurt like a sweet that's got stuck when you haven't chewed it properly.

Her throat ached with trying not to cry. If this was a story, Isla could put the book down and forget about their mission. Even Hermione couldn't do everything. When she couldn't get the hang of predicting the future, Hermione dropped out of Divination class. Isla couldn't get the hang of finding Mum, but she couldn't drop out from this mission.

She touched the cold lump in her pocket. Everything about her wanted to ignore it. Dread washed over her, a chill racing all the way from her neck through every vertebra to the bottom of her spine. She felt like a robot. Her stiff arms opened her jacket and the hand enclosing the clammy woollen bundle felt lifeless. In a dead voice she said,

'Gotta bury Weasley.'

They slithered off the rocks onto a stretch of wet sand. Lac sat on the sand with his head between his knees. Isla knelt next to him and rocked the woolly hat in her arms. Nothing worse could happen. Except the obvious.

Lac screeched, a piercing call that amplified through Isla's zinger, and caused a bolt of pain in her head. He scooped handfuls of hard sand, acting more like a ferret than a bird. Isla peeked inside the hat for a last look and laid it in the hole that Lac had made. The children held hands and knelt beside their pet's burial ground.

'Goodbye Weasley, old friend.'

Lac kissed his fingers and laid his palm on top of the wool.

Together, they slid the pile of sand back over the hole and pressed it down, almost as if they were making a sandcastle. Isla lay on top of the grave, trying to hug the cold sand.

'I can't believe he's gone,' she wailed. Violent hiccups rose from the bottom of her belly. As she lay there, moisture seeped through her clothes making her legs and tummy feel like ice. When she was wet through, she sat back on her knees, sniffed a huge snort and wiped away snot with her sleeve.

'Now there'll always be a piece of our family on this island,' she said. *So what? As if that helps anything.* She just wanted to lie down on that wet sand and close her eyes and leave everything to Hermione.

She stood up, bent her head against the breeze and walked towards the water. She trod carefully over an outcrop of jagged rocks, still sniffling, and stepped onto an expanse of bare beach. Wind whipped sand into her face and the harsh grains stung her skin. Millions of years ago these tiny particles were rocks, now they were just microscopic insignificant specks.

With Weasley gone, finding Mum seemed even more desperate.

Down at the water's edge, a line of pawprints disappeared into the shallow water. Signs that something had been here, and then was gone. Waves rolled forward and fizzled into zillions of little bubbles before sliding back into the sea. Isla watched in a half-trance. Wave after wave, nonstop, as if the sea's mission was to keep going, in and out, forever. Isla and Lac's mission was the opposite. They had to keep going, but surely it would end sometime.

The mission was all going wrong. They were no closer to finding where Mum had been, let alone where she was now. Instead of finding Mum they were lost on this island. If you get stuck, go back to the beginning and look again at the clues to find what you've missed. Those were the instructions in a toy detective kit Isla used to have. But this wasn't a little kid mission. Their whole lives depended on this. Whatever she was doing, they had to find her. They couldn't live without Mum.

CHAPTER 23

DESPAIR

Isla and Lac tried walking along the beach, but sharp rocks blocked their way, and beyond them the sea raged. Down near the shore, angry waves were frothing and throwing pebbles at the water's edge. They had to backtrack, and clamber back up onto the road.

'It's not gonna rain again, is it?'

Drops of moisture settled on Isla's coat as she plodded on, head down, along the road. Everything was moving fast. Patches of pea green light brightened the grassland as the sun slipped in and out of layers of cloud. The sea seemed to be racing to the shore, crashing its foaming breakers and retreating with a roar.

They looked for a shop amidst a cluster of buildings set back from the road. No shop, no food. The taste of Kayla's mum's meat'n'rice popped into Isla's mouth. No matter how many sweets they'd stuffed coming home from school, they always had room for her amazing cinnamon pudding.

'I wonder what we'll have to eat when we get there,' Isla said as the wind pushed drizzle into their faces.

'Cheepity?'

'Um, I'm not sure. I don't know where 'there' is yet. But we'll find it.'

But what if we don't? What if we never find Mum? We'd never be able to go home. Isla thought of her bedroom, SuperTed and all her books. And the secret things in her golden box. Lac picked the scab on his elbow, put it in his mouth, and fresh red blood oozed from his skin.

'I'm hungry too. I wish I hadn't thrown away that soggy bread.'

Fine rain was spitting everywhere.

'Looks like we'll have to find a place to shelter,' Isla said.

Plump raindrops soaked their hair before they could get their hoods up. Isla saw a movement in the grass. A furry animal like a miniature kangaroo stood upright, short arms tucked in front of its chest. Long ears twitching, it flattened its whole body and took off like a racing car, back legs leaping huge strides, and vanished into long grass.

She grabbed Lac's hand. 'Hey, our kid, that was a hare! If we were real warriors, we'd have caught it. And eaten it.'

They were words of hope that she didn't feel. Sounded like Mum talking when the fridge was nearly empty. *Anyway, how do you skin an animal?* She pushed a mass of wet hair under her hood and felt drips trickling down her neck.

Lac poked Isla's arm. "Mew-ew."

She was fed up with pretending to be cheerful.

"Jeez, Lac, stop all this bird stuff."

Lac roared, baring his gappy teeth, his fingers shaped into claws. Tears filled his eyes and rolled down his cheeks. He bashed her hard on her back, launching Luke Skywalker at her face and shrieked, 'Skreek! Skreek! Skreek!'

Isla grasped his wrists. 'Hey! Stop acting like a demon. Stop it!'

He wrenched free. Hot breath streamed from his nostrils, and his wild eyes darted about. His arms flew as if they were going to take off from his shoulder sockets. Isla grabbed his legs and they both fell onto the grass verge. Isla held tight onto his writhing body until it bucked one last time. He lay on his back, gasping and coughing. Blood glistened from the graze on his face, which he'd scraped again.

He started to choke so Isla pulled him into a sitting position and thumped him on the back.

'Don't be sick. Remember you're a Jedi knight, a member of the Resistance, like Luke Skywalker.' She held his shoulders.

The demon subsided. He wiped snot from his face, wincing when he brushed tears from his sore cheek. His face wore a sullen, wounded expression.

'I'm sorry, our kid. You've got to be brave.' Isla leant down and her hair fell into a curtain over him. 'We've both got to be brave. I can't be daring for both of us. I need you to be bold alongside me.'

A gust of wind blew the curtain aside. Isla picked up Luke Skywalker and twisted the figure's arms above its head.

'"To boldly go where no child has gone before",' she said.

Lac snatched his toy from her and held Luke in front of him. 'Cawwww, cawwww, cawwww.'

They heaved the rucksacks onto their backs and the wind pushed them along the road running next to the beach. The road went on for ages next to flat scrubby land. Lots of sheep but no people or cars. Yesterday she was sure they were on the right track. But as the day wore on, she replayed what the boy from the shop had said. He'd smirked when he said it. 'There's only the one road on this side of the island.'

The rain had turned into light drizzle. A dim glow covered everything. Brushing matted hair out of her eyes, Isla stared in the dusky light. Yesterday the sea was glittering but today it had disappeared into a blank haze. They had no option but to continue their trek, looking for any sign – anything – that Mum was still somewhere. The alternative was too horrible to think about.

Lac's feet were making a horrible scraping sound on the gravelly road, and his head sank towards his dragging shoes, making a headless long shadow behind him. A few minutes later he dropped to his knees and the weight of his rucksack rolled him onto his back. He was asleep on the grass by the roadside.

Isla cried. She pulled the jumbled-up tent out of her pack and pegged it out as best she could. The tears kept falling while she struggled. In the end she made a kind of wigwam, with its single pole poking out like a chicken leg, and hurled herself inside on her face, bawling. She crawled outside again, dragged her drowsy brother into the shelter of the wonky tent and flopped her own heavy limbs next to him.

There were no thoughts in her head as she plunged into sleep, just an infinite void like outer space. With no stars.

CHAPTER 24

RASPBERRIES AND CAKE

Isla opened her eyes to a blackness pricked with sparks of light.

'Isla.' Mum's voice had woken her.

'Mum?'

Drops of sweat trickled underneath her armpits, going cold on her skin. Isla sat up, panting, felt clammy earth under her sleeping bag.

'Mum?' she said again, knowing there'd be no answer, it was just a dream.

'Mum?' Maybe it was her ghost. Lac rustled in his sleeping bag with a faint screechy snore.

Isla gulped, but her mouth was dry, and she couldn't swallow. She tried to go back to sleep, but a mishmash of thoughts was bugging her. She lay with eyes staring into the darkness and a feeling of dread in her bones. Hermione Granger managed to protect her parents from evil. But could Isla do the same?

Faint rays began to appear through a gap above her in their makeshift shelter. Small tweets started up, followed by high-pitched shrills and rougher squawks from seagulls. Isla wanted to wake Lac, to find out what they were saying. Maybe they could see clues from up there that were invisible to humans down here.

Next time she woke, Lac's feet were disappearing through the opening in the hotch-potch mess of the tent. Sticking her head out, she saw him hopping from one foot to the other. "Irrip-irrip," he sang, an eager grin on his face. His cheek was looking better, blotched with pink skin where he'd picked the scabs.

'Morning, birdy,' she said as she fixed her zinger in place. 'What's making you so cheerful?'

No answer, of course. Isla lugged their gear out onto the grass and started pulling out pegs from the scrappy tent. Together, they rolled the cloth and pegs into a bundle and jammed it into her rucksack.

It must have rained again – the wet ground soaked their knees and the remnants of tent weighed heavily on her back when she shouldered her pack once more. Lac skittered ahead, hopping from clump to clump of grass in the middle of the road. Over distant islands, grey sheets of rain fell in smudges from dark rainclouds, but here it was dry, and directly overhead white puffy clouds made Isla feel strangely happy. They were so pretty, like candy floss in the blue sky.

While they walked, Isla imagined Mum standing on a beach, looking out to sea. Then she pictured her on top of a cliff, still gazing towards the horizon, with the black sheet of her hair flying like outstretched wings. She was here, somewhere, Isla knew it. But she didn't know why.

Archie had said, 'There's only the one road on this side of the island'. But the tarmac suddenly stopped. It was a dead end. Beyond a red letterbox sunk into a stone wall, a path led to a house which looked like it had been plonked at the end of the world. A mass of prickly bushes sprawled against the sunny stones, sprouting hundreds of small red berries.

'We must have come the wrong way. I knew that boy was lying.'

Isla and Lac crouched behind the wall and peeked out to check there were no adults spying on them. Lac ducked low, stretched out his arm and popped a raspberry in his mouth. Then another. And another. Isla picked three berries in quick succession. Compared with yesterday's stomach-full of gloopy raw egg, these tasted fabulous. An image burst into Isla's head of her and Kayla raiding a mass of tangled bushes next to the railway line at the edge of their local park.

Finger and thumb round a berry, Lac pulled hard, but he screwed up his face when he chewed it.

'Got a sour one? Don't pick the pale ones, they're not ripe.'

Isla gathered another handful of raspberries. 'Mmm, gorgeous. Try these. The juicy big ones are the sweetest.'

He chose the biggest, fattest berries in her outstretched palm, smiled his gap-toothy grin, and went back to the bush. Soon, their hands were stained red and covered in scratches. They hadn't noticed the bushes were pricking them while they gorged on the fruit.

'What're you doing?'

An old man appeared out of nowhere the other side of the gate. Lac and Isla jumped – they were so lost in stuffing raspberries into their mouths, they hadn't noticed him watching them.

'Eating raspberries,' Isla said. 'Why, are they yours?' Isla knew she shouldn't talk like this to an adult, but it was pretty obvious what they were doing. 'Sorry,' she said. 'I didn't mean to be rude.' *Manners, huh?*

He grunted the sort of 'humph' that grown-ups do when you say sorry.

'Are you hungry?' he asked and opened his gate.

They nodded. Alarm bells rang in Isla's head, but he seemed kind.

'Would you like a piece of my wife's cake?'

Before she could say no, Lac rushed through the gate and threw her an expectant look over his shoulder. They shouldn't go in a stranger's house, but she was so hungry.

'I can see you want some, lad. Come on then, the two of you.'

He took Lac's hand, and shouted through the open doorway,

'Annie, we've got visitors!' Turning to Isla, he waved her forward. 'Come on in, hen, leave your bags in the hallway.'

Isla did as she was told but kept her shoes on as he closed the front door behind her and ushered them into a room with a green and beige carpet. Its patterns looked like interlocking cul-de-sacs.

'Here you are children, take a seat,' the old man said, pulling out two chairs at a round table near the window.

He left the room and returned carrying plates, a teapot and glasses, followed by an old woman wearing an apron, pushing a trolley. Isla's mouth watered as she watched her unload two large plates, each boasting a home-made cake. The old man slid into his seat, and the old woman stood over them, wielding an enormous knife.

Isla's misgivings all disappeared as she crammed fruit cake into her mouth. Next, they had a slice of sponge cake filled with cream and icing on the top, crowned by a fake cherry plonked right in the centre. They slurped lemonade. This was heaven.

'Could you take another slice?' Mr Old Man asked, and without waiting for an answer, he piled up their plates again.

'Thank you,' Isla said.

'Peep-peep,' squeaked Lac, his mouth overflowing with crumbs.

'Can't he speak?' Mrs Old Woman asked.

Lac's head bobbed from side to side between Isla and her.

Isla swallowed her mouthful of amazing cake.

'Yes, of course he can. He's just – playing a game, seeing how long he can be –' Isla couldn't think of a word '– birdy.'

'Oh.' She paused, then said, 'Awful young to be camping on your own, aren't you?'

CHAPTER 25

CAPTURED

How did she know they were alone? 'We're not on our own. We're meeting our mum.'

'Aye, that's what Grizelda said.'

'Grivvelda?' Isla mumbled through a gooey mess of sponge and cream. Was Mrs Old Woman a witch? Her grey hair hung in a ponytail down her back, not scooped up in a bun like Professor McGonagall. And her cheeks were smoother, not nearly as puckered and lined.

'At the Co-op by the harbour. She said two children were looking for their ma.'

'Archie said they were barmy,' Mr Old Man said. 'Are you?'

'No, er – .' Isla looked out of the window. 'Actually, our mum's out picking raspberries for our tea,' she said in a rush.

'Is she now?' Mrs Oldie said in that mocking way when adults don't believe you.

Now Isla looked more closely, the old woman's lips squeezed into a disapproving frown exactly like Professor McGonagall.

'Yes, in fact we'd better go, she'll be waiting for us.'

'And where will she be waiting?'

The lips tightened, leaving only a tiny streak of red lipstick on show.

'Out there.' Isla waved her hand towards the back of the house, where the island met the sea.

'Out there?'

Isla's fingers felt sticky with icing, but she didn't dare lick them.

'Yes,' she said. Lac nodded like the black-headed gulls that had been wading in the shallows yesterday.

'By the sea?'

'That's right.'

'On the rocks?' Those pinched lips hardly opened.

'Well, no not exactly.'

Mr Old Man leaned forward as if he was trying to help. 'Further round…..?' His gentle tone was unbearable, it made Isla's throat ache.

'Yes, further round.'

'At the bottom of the cliffs? Is your mother a seal, by any chance?' He sat up straight and folded his arms.

Isla looked at her grimy shoes, caked with sand.

'You poor wains.' Mrs Oldie's blue-veined hand pressed on top of Isla's filthy fingers. 'I don't think you're meeting her. You don't know where she is, do you?' Isla cringed inside at the menacing tone in her voice.

Mr Oldie got to his feet. 'I'll get on the phone,' he said, and left the room.

Isla ran her hands through her knotty hair. *Hermioneeeeee. What now? We can't stay here. They'll stop us finding Mum.*

'No need to look so miserable,' Mrs Oldie said. 'We'll get you cleaned up in no time. If your mum's not around, I'm sure your dad can pick you up.' She winked, crinkling the skin around her eyes.

We've got to get out of here.

Isla said to Lac. 'Show Mrs Ol- I mean the nice lady your Luke Skywalker.' She wiggled on her chair. 'Can I go to the toilet?'

Down the corridor, as she passed the middle room, she heard Mr Oldie on the phone. 'If she can't come until the next boat over, yes we'll keep them.'

Keep us? Prisoners?

Isla needed to implant a false memory charm into the old couple so they forgot all about her and Lac. *Don't be stupid. That's just stories, this is real.*

She stood with her good ear next to the slightly open door.

'We're both very well thank you...... And how are you all keeping?........ I expect Duncan's practising for the sheepdog trials.....' She heard lots of 'Mmm' and 'I think so' and 'yes, well....'

Isla skipped through the kitchen and into the bathroom at the end. She flushed the toilet. 'Do something,' she muttered to her dirty face in the mirror.

As Isla opened the bathroom door, Mrs Oldie was waiting on the other side, holding Luke Skywalker. 'Don't forget to give your hands a good wash.'

She looked down at Luke. 'We'll sort them out,' she muttered.

Next to her, Lac tried nicely to take him back, but Mrs Oldie wouldn't let go. They were trapped, and it was like Mrs Oldie was holding him hostage.

'Susan's not free to come and get you for a wee while,' called Mr Oldie from the middle room.

'Susan?' Isla asked.

'Our polis for these islands. She's busy over the water just now,' Mrs Oldie said.

'What's 'polis'?'

'Police.' Mrs Oldie sniffed, wrinkled her nose, and looked at Isla's scratched arms and filthy hands, and down at her torn jeans. 'Why don't I run you a bath?'

She squeezed past Isla into the bathroom and handed out a couple of towels from a cupboard.

'Just slip your clothes off, and I'll pop them in the washer for you. This wee toy could do with a bit of a shampoo too. Here you go, bonnie boy,' she said, laying Luke in the sink. She bent to turn on the bath taps, pouring a generous dollop of bubble bath into the rushing water. Out of the corner of her eye Isla caught a sneaky shadow. Lac, on his knees, reached up and swiped Luke, and bolted back into the corridor.

'Um, I'll just go in the kitchen to get undressed,' Isla said to Mrs Oldie's back, who was busy frothing the bubbles into a soapy foam.

'Oh-ho. Shy are we?' she called behind her. 'All right, dearie. Don't be long.'

'Smells lovely,' Isla said as she backed out, looking over her shoulder at Lac on tiptoes, squeezing open the latch on the front door.

Through the middle room door Mr Oldie said, 'Aye well, goodbye then.'

The door began to open. 'Annie,' he called. Then he spotted Isla. 'Hey, you!' In three strides, his hand seized Isla's shoulder as she leapt for the door that Lac had flung open. His thumbs dug into Isla's flesh.

'Oh no you don't, missy, everyone's out looking for you. You've caused too much trouble already.'

Trouble! 'Ow! Let go!' *We're in trouble alright.*

'Now where's that shifty little brother of yours?'

His glance took in the open door.

'He's gone. I've got to go. I'm supposed to look after him,' Isla screamed.

'You won't be going anywhere, dearie. The polis are looking for you.' He turned Isla round and kicked the front door closed.

'At least we've got one of the little devils,' he shouted to his wife.

She came out of the bathroom, wiping her hands on a towel. Her face looked like thunder. She held the door open.

'In you go.'

'I don't want a bath.'

Yes, you do.'

'I don't. I've got to find my brother.'

She took hold of Isla's wrist and shoved her into the bathroom, closing the door with a thump.

'You're having a bath whether you want it or not,' she said from the other side.

Isla almost fell into the bath. As she regained her balance, a key clicked. She banged on the door.

'I've got to find him,' she screamed.

'Leave that to me. I'm not a retired polis-man for nothing,' the old man shouted.

'Let me out!' she yelled. She was terrified to think of Lac out there on his own.

Isla let the plug out of the bath and the water sucked away with a horrible sound. She rattled the door again.

The front door slammed.

For once, she couldn't think how Hermione might help. *Even heroes don't know everything.* She screamed until she was hoarse, and her throat felt like she'd swallowed broken glass. Finally, she slumped down onto the toilet seat. If only she could play her trumpet, the music would be sure to soothe her. She closed her eyes. A vague thought scratched at the back of her mind. That news programme had jogged a memory, something about campaigners, not like Greta Thunberg's followers. Adult protesters.

That camp where Mum met Dad… The power station protest… Against polluting the atmosphere… burning coal, fossil fuel. Carbon emissions. Must have been dangerous if the police were there. Was Dad one of the jailed protesters in prison?

Isla got it. No Planet B meant there's only one planet, and the protesters' mission is to save it. End of. Like her and Lac's mission, Plan A was to find Mum, and there wasn't a plan B. They just had to find her. End of.

She stood up again, and banged and kicked the door until her fists hurt. She shouted, but no-one heard.

CHAPTER 26

ESCAPE

From a tiny hideout deep inside the raspberry bush, Lac heard a door open and crash shut. Faint wails from his sister inside the house made him clench his fists.

The voice of their captor reached him. 'Sure she won't get out?'

'No, Hector, she's locked in.' He heard a jangle of keys. 'I've turned the key in the front door as well.'

'Right then, this won't take long. He won't have got far.'

Two car doors slammed, an engine revved, and the car drove past Lac's hiding place. Scratched and bleeding, he pulled himself out and legged it across the road. Racing through machair flowers and grasses, he headed for a distant fringe of wild scrubby bushes.

Beating back ferns with a curved stick, Lac slogged uphill. Isla's plan for their mission wasn't working, so it was up to him now. The fact that he'd escaped showed how brilliant he was. But they still needed to find Mum. Luke's head stuck out of the pocket of his joggers like a warrior. Even though his sword was so small, he would help Lac keep them safe from invading foes. His bird friends had been doing a stunning job of watching out for enemies, except for just before. Hooding his eyes, Lac looked up to the sky.

'Craark?'

There was no answering cry.

'Craark,' he repeated.

A red and white helicopter circled around the cliffs at the end of the island.

He cupped his hands round his mouth and tried some other calls. 'Squew-ew.' Pause. 'Skreeek.' Pause. 'Aaaarwrkk.'

High up near the clouds, a distant call responded.

'Aaaarwrkk.' Then another, and another, until six or more crows wheeled in the air above him. They were back.

It would be better to rescue Isla from the dark side when the evil ones were asleep. In the meantime, he needed to lie low. Stay away from the road.

'Peep-peep.' The orange beak sounded a warning. Lac ducked. The ferns were as tall as him and provided good cover, but that helicopter was too close for comfort. He squeezed into dense bracken and came out at the bottom of a cliff, where a dark hole gaped. On his tummy, he wriggled towards the opening and slipped inside the shadow cast by the cave's entrance.

From this vantage point, he spotted a low stone cabin with slitty windows huddled on a piece of flat land surrounded by bracken.

'Aaaarwrkk,' the crows called again and again, circling over the hut.

He edged backwards, dropping onto all fours as he turned and retreated into long grass outside the cave. Stooping low, he disappeared back into the tall ferns. The helicopter droned overhead, wheeled round and receded into the distance.

The stone hut stood on its own in a clearing. Lac crawled towards it, peered through the open doorway, and crept inside. The earth floor was cold on his hands and damp seeped through the knees of his trousers. As his eyes got used to the gloom a blanket came into view, and a holdall.

'Peep-peep.' A warning sounded from above. He dived out through the door and into a patch of long grass.

The bracken swayed in time to the sound of steps. Something was coming up a hidden path. He inched forward on his hands and knees. A yellow and black insect with a tail as long as his finger hung upside down on a grass stalk, swaying almost level with his nose. Above the ferns, Lac glimpsed a human head, face lowered. The insect's wings whirred like a rocket engine revving up for lift-off. As the person emerged from the bracken, the dragonfly opened its transparent wings and swooped upwards. The human lifted her head to watch the fly-past.

Lac stood up.

"Ee-ee-ee," he shrieked, waving Luke Skywalker.

The human stopped. Screamed.

She opened and closed her mouth like a goldfish.

'Is it –? How? When–?'

Lac bolted forwards and crashed into Mum's middle, clasping his hands behind her back as if he was fixing himself there permanently. He howled and screeched. He let go long enough to lean back and make sure it really was her.

'Your cheek! What happened, our kid?' she cried.

He went back to holding her tight, pressing his cheek against her front.

She prised them gently apart and he showed her his bloody elbow. Mum held it with both hands and kissed it. She bent and looked into his green eyes, deep grooves furrowed into her forehead.

'Isla?'

'Skreek!'

The high-pitched squeal vibrated in Mum's skull.

'No!'

Her shriek triggered a fresh bout of wailing from Lac. Mum's arm folded round him like a protective wing.

'We came to find you,' he burst out. 'You were MISSING. And Isla's been CAPTURED. We've got to RESCUE her.'

CHAPTER 27

REALISING

Isla could hear muffled voices. She put her good ear to the keyhole. The television blared from the open living room door. *Left it on, stupid old cow,* she thought. They must be deaf to have it on so loud. A feeble grin floated on Isla's lips. *Like me.*

'The missing Birmingham children are believed to be on the island of Mora in the Outer Hebrides, where a search operation is underway,' a deep voice announced. She sagged, like a bouncy castle that sprang a leak. How did they know that?

'And in other news…'

It was that news story about the climate protesters again. Now it was a woman talking. Isla pressed her ear to the door even harder.

'He deceived me, I was in a very fragile state. I felt I was in a little bubble where nothing was real.' Isla drew in a sharp breath. 'I couldn't cope, it still keeps me awake at night.'

Something about the way she talked sounded like Mum. Having stuff on her mind that kept her awake. Except Mum did cope. Or did she? Isla never thought of Mum as fragile, but the bit about the bubble rang a bell. She tuned in to the TV voices again.

'You never suspected?' the man asked.

'My husband was a trained liar who became a nameless stranger overnight. He had a fake driving licence and passport,' the invisible woman said. 'He had a van, and used to offer people lifts after meetings, so he could find out where they lived.'

Mum, Isla and SuperTed in Dad's van. *Stop thinking about Dad,* Isla told herself. *Just because he was a delivery driver doesn't mean anything. It's Mum who's important.* Isla tasted blood where she'd chewed the inside of her cheek. *How am I going to find her? And now Lac's gone, too.*

She threw the old couple's toothbrush mug against the wall and stamped on a plastic bottle of shampoo which burst, oozing gooey green liquid. The bath panel cracked with the force of her angry kick. She climbed up to the window and pulled its lever back and forth with a fury she'd never ever felt before, until it came off in her hand. With all her strength, she lifted the bin over her head and smashed it against the frame until the wood split and the window hung open on one hinge. On tiptoe, she peered out, but she'd never fit through that gap, and outside it was a steep drop to the grass below.

There were no tears left. Her eyelids were drooping. She curled up in the bath amidst the toothbrush mug's scummy spit and shattered pieces of hard plastic and pulled the towel over her.

Arms over her face, eyes closed, she didn't sleep exactly, more like going into suspended animation, which was disturbed by a scuffling at the front door and the voices of her captors floating down the corridor.

'Can't believe we didn't find him,' Mr Oldie said.

'Little beggar. Hope he doesn't turn up in a ditch,' his wife said.

The man's voice softened. 'No, Annie, we don't want that. Let's pray the polis track him down.'

Isla felt desperate. She had to look for Lac, didn't matter if it took all night. She struggled out of the bath and banged on the door.

'Let me out!'

'Quiet, you!' boomed through the solid wood.

A few minutes later, the old woman unlocked the door and shoved a plate of beans on toast inside.

'He'll turn up, they've got the helicopter out looking for him,' she said, before locking the door again. 'These city kids – can't trust them an inch,' she announced loudly for Isla's benefit as she walked through the kitchen and slammed the living room door. That phrase 'city kids' stung, as if Isla was some unwanted low life.

CHAPTER 28

BREAKOUT

In Isla's prison, cold air flooded through the broken window. Shouting and gunfire erupted from the other end of the house, sounding like someone was being murdered on TV. She huddled in the bath, curled up like a lamb gaining warmth from its mother, but for Isla there was no mother and no warmth. Although she was desperately worried about Lac after the Oldies had returned empty-handed, she also felt triumphant that he had evaded capture. A trumpet fanfare in her head sang *Yay, buddy, good for you!* But as soon as she had this thought, her joy drained away. He could be in real danger.

A noise outside the bathroom window interrupted her thoughts.

'Chirrupy-cheep.'

Isla felt like she was inside one of those unreal bubbles. She'd recognize Lac's tweets anywhere. Was she dreaming? She stood up and touched the tiled wall. She was definitely awake. A stick tapped on the broken window frame. She climbed onto the edge of the bath, and nearly fell back into it when she saw who was outside.

Her tongue was too big for her mouth. Her eyelids felt super-heavy and she'd lost control of her limbs - each movement took an age.

'Shhh. We're breaking you out, babs.' *Babs!*

She yearned to fall into Mum's outstretched arms. Easier said than done when you're locked in a bathroom and trying to wriggle through a window that's too small for you to get through, and Mum's standing on a wheelie bin pulling your arms out of their sockets, whispering,

'Nearly there, our kid.'

But you can't scream when splinters from the broken window-frame stick into your hip, and *scrrrrch!* your jacket rips. And you definitely can't give up.

Us city kids go all out for what we want, Isla thought while her legs waved around in the air and her front hung perilously over the gap between the wheelie bin and the ground. Lac stood below, arms thrust upwards to catch her when –

– heaving, hauling, thighs and knees and shins scraping, she slithered and splatted on top of Mum. Lac was squashed under her legs, with the overturned wheelie bin spilling rubbish all over them.

They didn't wait to hear the old man come to investigate the noise. No way was he going to think that a deer had knocked over the bin, and he'd see the broken window straight away. They ran.

They were a hundred metres down the road by the time they heard his shouts, and crouching the other side of a wall, panting, when the old couple's car swept past. They were in a graveyard. A maze of gravestones and crosses stood in front of a broken-down church. Leaning against the rough stone of the wall, at last Isla could turn to Mum.

She rested her head on Mum's shoulder, knocking her glasses wonky. Inhaling Mum's familiar smell, she nuzzled her collarbone. Shakes overwhelmed Isla, and great noisy gulps came out of her mouth.

'I knew you were here,' she blubbered into Mum's shirt. 'You were gone. We had to come and find you.' She cried and snorted until snot smeared all over her torn jacket. Mum squeezed her so tight she could hardly breathe.

'My babbies, what's happened? Where's Lou?'

'She's – ' Isla tried to think through the fog. '– in hospital. Operation.'

Mum's grip tightened on her shoulder.

'Same day you left,' Isla mumbled.

Horror flooded Mum's face. 'Who's been looking after you?'

'Just us.'

For some reason Isla felt like she'd done something wrong, and Mum was about to tell her off.

'No-one?' Mum's voice sounded far away. 'You didn't tell Uncle Dave?' She wasn't letting Isla off the hook.

Isla shook her head. 'I didn't know till I found your note.'

'But why are you here?'

'I told you – we had a mission. To find you,' blurted Lac, burrowing under Mum's armpit, making her put her arm round him.

Isla stared at him. He stared back.

'What? Can't I talk now? You said, 'Don't say a word'. But we've finished our mission.' He looked up at Mum. 'We found Mum.'

'You came to look for me?' Mum asked. 'Alone?'

Isla nodded. *Obviously.*

'You didn't tell any grown-ups? How did you –?'

'Mum, please don't get cross. Didn't you see my missed calls?'

Mum looked blank.

Isla sat up and faced her. 'You didn't call or text us.'

'I deleted my WhatsApp. Then I lost my phone somewhere, the ship I think,' Mum replied.

Lac prodded Isla, and when she didn't speak, he said, 'We had to find you. We sneaked in your room. Isla found a ring like that.' He pointed to a stone cross with a circle. Now he was gabbling, he couldn't stop. 'And we spied on your computer.'

Isla felt the jolts of her hiccups knocking into Mum, who was shivering violently.

'I used the emergency credit card. Me and our kid got the camping gear from the loft. I found that ring,' Isla babbled on. 'I hoped it would lead us to you, but I lost it.'

Something wet dripped into her hair. Mum was crying.

Lac fiddled underneath Luke Skywalker's trousers, twisting his fingers around Luke's leg. With a shy look, he produced an object between his thumb and forefinger. 'Look, Mum.'

'You!' Isla said. 'What are you playing at?'

He held the ring out to Mum and replied to Isla. 'I gave it to Luke for protection in case you lost it again. It was leading us to Mum.'

Isla uttered a stifled screech through clenched teeth.

'Your dad gave me that ring,' Mum said in a faraway voice. 'He told me to keep it a secret, and never wear it.'

She made no move to take it from Lac, so Isla reclaimed it.

The three of them sat for a long time, almost lifeless, like a heartbroken living statue. Frozen.

CHAPTER 29

NAMES

Upright gravestones cast long shadows in the evening light. A high-up bird squeaked like Isla's first efforts on the trumpet. Why wasn't Mum happy to see them?

'Come on, Lac. Best to leave her for a little bit,' Isla said, biting her lip. They got up and slowly backed away.

Lac whispered, 'She won't disappear, will she?'

'No.' But Isla was worried. Mum had gone into a blank space. Kicking at stones in the path, she mooched around, keeping her eye on Mum's hunched figure by the wall. Twisting between the gravestones, blurry names and dates from a hundred years ago reeled in front of her eyes. She reached out a finger and stroked a crust of spiky pale green lichen creeping over the top of a curved stone. Although it felt dead, she knew it must be alive since it was a plant.

'It's really spooky in here.' Her words fell flat. No-one answered.

The grey, yellow and pink of the gravestones looked pretty, which was weird in a place full of dead bodies and skeletons. A cross with a circle stood above many graves. Isla blinked. Same cross. Same circle. Same swirly decorative shapes as the ring that was now safely back on her thumb.

'This feels like a secret place. It's so quiet, almost as if something's hidden here.'

The bird above uttered more tiny squeaks. Lac echoed its call and followed it with a gentle 'Coo-oo-oo.'

'Back in birdy-land are you? I know what you mean, it feels really peaceful. But it's almost as if bad things happened and have been buried here with the people under the ground.'

Isla chewed her thumb. 'Underground,' she muttered.

She had never met anyone else called MacLean. Looking at the gravestones, she saw their name everywhere. 'All these families have got our name,' she said.

Lac stood in front of a clean gravestone, his eyes fixed on the words carved into it. The name. *Lachlan MacLean.* Her stomach turned over.

'My name,' he whispered.

Isla looked at Lac, her Lachlan. She read the words out loud. *'Lachlan MacLean aged 64. Lost at sea. Drowned in a storm.'*

Lac gulped. 'Lost at sea. Drowned.'

It didn't make sense. Lachlan MacLean was standing next to her. *Lachlan MacLean drowned in a storm.* Isla imagined being lost at sea. What if the ship they'd come on had got lost in fog and they'd never arrived? Words from that woman on the TV crowded into her head.

'With a missing person, you're always in limbo. Like a ship lost in the fog,' she'd said. Not drowned, just floating around forever and never rescued.

Lac took Isla's hand, and a tremor passed between them. They found three more Lachlan MacLeans and several *Alexander (Sandy) MacLeans* who had died. Like Dad. But Dad had died in a motorbike crash in Birmingham. Lac squatted next to each one, tracing his finger over the letters and placing his hand flat on the grassy grave.

Isla was miffed that there were no Isla MacLeans.

'Why all these Lachlans? Have they got anything to do with us?' Lac asked.

A few had been lost at sea. Underneath their names and dates there was more lettering: *'Gus am bris an là.'* She scratched her head. 'What's that?'

Some said '*Dadaidh*' or '*Mamaidh*'.

'Maybe that means Dad? Mum?' Isla said.

They squatted at the edge of a low wall around a miniature child's grave. Isla read the tiny gravestone. *'McCluskey, aged 6. Our little Andy gone to the angels.'*

'Hang on a sec.' Why did that ring a bell?

Mum appeared from nowhere and stood silently behind them. Her hand flew to her mouth. She walked away and sat on a bench, elbows on knees and head in her hands, and called to them in a shaky voice from behind her curtain of hair.

'Can you leave me alone for a few minutes, duckies?'

'Okay, Mum.'

But nothing was okay. Isla re-read the inscription on the child's grave.

'Loved forever by Mamaidh and Dadaidh. Gus am bris an là.'

She'd heard that name before. Andy McCluskey. Something weird was happening. It felt like an invisible beetle was crawling up her spine. Something about children who'd died. That man on the TV in the caravan had said,

'... stole the names of dead children for their fake identity.'

Then the woman had spoken:

'In the end, I pretended he'd died, just for my own peace of mind. And for our child.'

It could have been Mum talking, but it was a total stranger.

'Child?' the interviewer asked.

'We had a baby.' Pause. 'I still can't accept that everything about him was fake.'

That baby's dad had a fake name.

They walked back to Mum, and Lac peered under the hair covering her face, then made Luke Skywalker gesture to the gate at the far end of the cemetery.

'Luke says we've got to get out of here. The enemy will return.'

Isla felt dazed. Mum shook herself and took Lac's hand.

'You're right. Come on, duckies.'

The sun had dropped low over the sea and slid away out of sight. Shadows were gone, replaced by a gloom that was neither light nor dark. They followed Mum through the gate and across a strip of machair.

CHAPTER 30

HUT

They walked single file along a path splattered with sheep's poo, leading uphill into a wilderness of those huge thorny bushes with yellow flowers.

'Where are we going?' Isla asked from her position at the back.

'To Mum's hideout,' Lac replied.

'Mum's got a hideout?'

Lac bashed his chest with his fist. 'I *know*.'

Too confused to ask any more questions, Isla followed her mum and brother along a narrow path between the prickly plants, and beyond into tall bracken curving over Lac's head. She wiped moisture from her face. *More rain,* she thought, *but I don't care anymore.* She walked like an automaton through the drizzle. It was dry underfoot – the ferns protected them from the worst of the rain.

The path came to an end, and Isla emerged onto flat grass surrounded by bracken. Mum stood in the low doorway of a stone hut, waving them inside.

'Her hideout,' Lac said.

Isla stumbled through the entrance into a dark space that smelt of soil and mould. But it had a roof and it was dry.

'Welcome to my palace,' Mum said.

Isla stood in the middle of the room until her eyes adjusted to the dim light and she could pick out details of her surroundings. Two crumpled blankets. A sleeping mat. Orange plastic bag. Some empty food containers in a heap in the corner.

Mum laid out a blanket on top of the mat on the floor opposite a grimy window.

'Is there any food in here?' Isla asked, poking her nose inside the plastic bag. She rummaged amongst empty packets and found a pasty. Sitting on the mat next to Mum and Lac, she ripped open the plastic cover and sank her teeth into the pastry. She tore off a huge chunk overflowing with meat and potato and passed the rest to Lac. His cheeks bulged as he chomped a huge bite and pressed the remainder to Mum's lips. She nibbled a corner and handed it back to Isla, who stuffed the last piece into her mouth.

'Now, you've got some explaining to do,' Mum said.

Isla's head cleared. She spoke through her half-eaten mouthful. 'Excuse me, Mum. *You've* got some explaining to do.' The pasty was a sticky mess in her mouth, muffling her words.

For some reason, they all laughed.

'Oh babs, it's so good to have you back. My precious kiddies. I missed you every second.'

She wiped tears of joy from the corners of her eyes and pulled both her children into a massive hug. She stroked Isla's hair and began inspecting Lac's neck and wrists, wincing at his scratches and scabs. He snatched his hands away and jumped up in the middle of the room.

'You never guessed we'd come on a mission, did you, Mum?' He danced from foot to foot, yelling at the top of his voice. 'We went on a train and a ship and told lies to grown-ups (sorry, Mum), then we got caught and I escaped, and I FOUND YOU! Not just me – ' he broke off and fell to his knees, groping under the blanket, then leapt up again ' – Luke looked for you too.'

'Thanks a bunch,' Isla said.

'Well, you couldn't, you were in prison.' He sat cross-legged in front of Mum. 'Luke hid from the enemies,' he explained, 'so he didn't get discovered by people wanting to destroy our mission.'

'Were you out in that storm the other night?' Mum asked. They nodded.

'Where did you sleep?'

'An old boat. The tent's ruined,' Isla said to the muddy floor between her knees.

'There's something else, isn't there? What is it, chuck?' Mum asked, looking into her eyes. 'You're really miserable.'

Isla couldn't face her. 'We lost Weasley.'

'Weasley?'

'We couldn't leave him behind. He came with us on the train and ship. He died in that storm – in a massive puddle.' Isla scrunched into a ball and sobbed. Between hiccups, she tried to force out more words but Lac did it for her.

'We buried him on the beach.'

Holding herself round her middle, Mum leant forward and spoke as if her arms were a snake squeezing her. 'I'm so sorry. It's all my fault.' She had never talked like this before. Isla didn't know what to say; she sat scratching the bites on her arms. Mum kissed each of them on the top of their heads and drew in a breath.

Several breaths. Her eyes were fixed on the greying light filtering through the window, and she sucked in another lungful of air to start speaking.

She broke the silence. 'I came here to find out about Dad and his family.'

'Dadaidh,' Lac whispered.

CHAPTER 31

ABOUT DAD

'I'm not supposed to tell you …'

'Mum!' Isla wriggled round so they were face-to-face.

'... but I can't live in this....' she closed her eyes and opened them again, '... this limbo.' She ran her fingers through her hair.

Limbo. The invisible woman's words.

'What's limbo?' Lac asked.

Mum thought for a moment. 'Being stuck in not knowing. Seven years of being stuck. I knew your dad came from this island, so I thought I might find something about him here.'

Wind blew under the gap in the door. Lac jammed his thumb in his mouth. A huge lump in Isla's throat almost stopped her next question, which came out in a tiny voice.

'He came from here?' Something didn't make sense. 'You've been on a mission to find Dad? Did you find anything?'

'No, ducky.'

Lac burst out, 'But our mission was to find *you*. You could have fallen off a cliff. You might be DEAD. Or eaten by a wild animal.'

Mum's tiny smile left sadness in her eyes. Isla wanted to shake her. Outside, a lamb bleated for its mum.

'Did you re-trace Dadaidh's steps?' Lac asked. His gaze focused on Luke Skywalker on his lap, his small fingers sliding the lightsaber in and out of Luke's gloved fist.

Mum dipped her head. 'I was looking for his family, so I could ask what happened to him after he disappeared.'

The tiny lightsaber whisked to and fro.

Isla rubbed her eyes with her knuckles. Some things weren't adding up. Or maybe they were. It was getting dark, hard to see Mum's face. Lac's head drooped. They pulled a blanket around their shoulders and snuggled in closer to each other. The three of them, just like always. Not quite always.

'Mum, what's the secret?'

Names kept running through Isla's mind. Lachlan, Sandy, MacLean. Her brother, her dad, dead strangers. What was the connection? Why had Mum called Dad a different name? She called him Mac, and then said Andy, not Sandy. Not MacLean.

'Kids, your dad was....he was....,' she started.

'We know. A climate protester,' Isla said. 'Did you know David Attenborough?'

'Not likely.' She smiled for a moment, and the worry lines eased slightly. 'He's far too famous. I'm just a nobody.'

'But there's something more, isn't there?'

Lac nestled closer to Mum and his eyes slid shut.

Mum made a pillow with her coat, laid Lac down on the sleeping mat, and tucked the other blanket around him. She kissed his forehead.

'Sleep tight, little feller.'

She sat back and put her arm round Isla's shoulder. 'You've been so brave,' Mum said.

'Have we? I don't feel brave. We just had to do it. There was no alternative.' Another Greta Thunberg phrase.

'Luke was brave,' Lac mumbled from under his blanket.

Isla couldn't leave it. She shivered and pulled the blanket closer around her knees.

'Was Dad arrested, in trouble with the police?'

Red blotches appeared on Mum's cheeks and her lips quivered. She did that throat-clearing grunt that adults do. Then she told Isla something she could never have guessed.

'Your Dad didn't die in a motorbike crash.'

Her voice grew louder. 'We were happy together.' She took Isla's hands in hers. 'After you were born, I didn't want to protest any more. But Dad carried on.' She paused. 'You were nearly two when he disappeared the first time.'

Mum shook her head from side to side. 'How could he leave us?'

Isla punched her arm. 'How could *you* leave *us?*'

Mum stared at the dark window. 'He said he had to go away, I didn't know where. He texted every week, and then – nothing.'

She picked at her fingers and shook her head. Shuffling down into a lying position on the floor, she held out the blanket for Isla to join her. The wind was moaning outside, but here inside it felt safe. It was so familiar, lying on Mum's chest and stretching her arm over her tummy. Mum started speaking again.

'I thought he'd left me. Us. But the next year he came back. On your birthday.'

'How old was I?'

'Three.'

'Was he still hiding from the police?'

'Yes. But he said he loved us, couldn't stay away.' She stroked Isla's hair. 'I thought we were back together. We even went on a protest again. Dad grew a beard and wore fake glasses so the police wouldn't recognize him.'

Isla recalled the rasp of Dad's unshaven cheek, his massive hands holding hers, calling her a bonnie girl and swinging her round until she was dizzy.

'I remember sleeping in a tent and playing with other kids.'

Mum chuckled. 'We had to tell you off for making guns out of the wire we'd cut from the power station fence. We believed in peace and nonviolence and our children were shooting each other.'

Power station – of course.

'One day, I picked you both up from Aunty Lou's as usual. But when I came home, he'd gone again. I've never heard from him since.'

'No texts?'

'No.'

'Where did he go?'

'Haven't a clue.'

'He's not dead?'

There was a long silence. Isla's head moved up and down with Mum's breathing.

'I don't know. You kept asking. In the end, I told you he'd died, to stop you pestering me about where he was, when I didn't know. I convinced myself that maybe he really had died.' Isla could feel Mum's voice vibrating in her chest. 'I never knew for sure. It plagues me.'

Isla lifted her head but Mum pushed it gently back down. 'That's enough for now, ducky. Time for sleep.'

Isla lay staring into the dark for ages. She guessed Mum wasn't asleep either.

'Mum.'

'Mmmm?'

'Did we ever go to the seaside with Dad?'

'Just that power station camp in Wales.'

'I can remember it. The smell of the seaweed.'

'That was the last one I went to.' Mum turned over on her side with her back to Isla.

The rain rattled on the corrugated iron roof as Isla re-ran the conversation over and over in her head. A turmoil of questions whirled so fast that she couldn't put them into words. Eventually, the irregular patter of drops became a blur as she dropped into sleep.

CHAPTER 32

HELICOPTER

The helicopter had been droning overhead since early morning, firstly out at sea, then circling over the island. Isla had an uneasy feeling that it was pursuing them, and they were its prey. Round and round it orbited in the sky, hunting like an eagle with evil eyes whose deadly beak and sharp talons were ready to snatch a rabbit. But unlike a rabbit, Isla, Lac and Mum couldn't scurry underground to hide.

'What are we going to do, Mum?'

'I dunno, babs.'

Isla glared back at her but didn't say anything about 'babs'. She sat up and shuffled next to Mum, who was sitting beside sleeping Lac. Cold seeped up from the earth floor.

'Are you in trouble too, Mum?'

'I might be, for leaving you.' There were dark shadows under her eyes, as if she hadn't slept all night.

Isla hugged her arms around her middle, trying to find a bit of warmth. 'There was a boy in the shop who said he'd seen you, I thought he was trying to help, but he tricked us. Must have been his idea of fun.'

Mum grimaced. 'I really don't know what to do now. When I got here, I thought people would help me find out about Mac. But nobody seemed to want to talk.'

Mum spoke as if Isla was a grown-up. Isla scratched her millionth bite, and a bead of blood popped out on her wrist. She dared to ask a question that was bugging her.

'Was he Mac or Sandy?'

Mum shot the answer straight back. 'He was both.' Not like her usual vague replies.

Isla wrinkled her eyebrows. 'What, Sandy on Mondays and Mac on Tuesdays?'

'No, I knew him as Mac, but later he told me his real name was Sandy.'

'Weird. How can someone have two names?' Isla was cold, but there was no warmth coming from Mum's body.

'Mac is a nickname for lots of Scottish people whose surname begins with Mac....'

Yet another thing Isla never knew until now. This mission was turning into a proper learning expedition.

'....and Sandy is short for Alexander. Also for people with red hair. Mac – Sandy – was both.'

Lac's eyes popped open. He sat up and threw the blanket aside. 'Cool. I could be called Sandy.'

He got up and heaved open the door of the hut, head cocked backwards as he strained to see the helicopter.

'Wow. A rescue 'copter.' Its tail reminded him of the whirring dragonfly he'd seen yesterday. The helicopter turned in a great arc round the mountain and returned into full view, its bulbous body flying low over the dense bracken.

'Lac! Shut the door!' Mum yelled.

He pushed the heavy door closed and stood with his back to it. 'Why?'

A disembodied male voice filled the air. Above the deafening whirr of the rotor blades, fuddled words streamed from the helicopter's loudspeaker.

'ISLA, LACHLAN. Show us where you are. We'll rescue you.'

'What was that?' Isla asked.

'I heard it too,' Mum said.

'What did it say? Tell me.'

Mum repeated the words. Lac crawled on hands and knees under the window – as if anyone could see through the crusted-up grimy glass. Mum reached for a bottle of water, passed it to Isla and then took a swig herself, and gave it to Lac.

He curled into Mum's lap, sucking his thumb again. 'Why are we hiding? We've found you. Can't we go home now?'

The noise of the helicopter grew fainter. Isla cracked open the door and saw it hovering above the caves in the mountain cliff face. She turned back to Mum.

'Is this where you've been staying all the time?'

'No, babs. I was with a lady called Mrs MacDonald for a couple of days. Everyone seems to be called Mac-Something on this island. But she treated me like an outsider, wouldn't tell me anything.' Mum picked at some loose skin around her little fingernail. 'I'd drawn a blank after coming all this way. But I couldn't leave, there was something I still didn't understand….'

'May the Force be with you,' Lac lisped '*Forth*' around the thumb in his mouth.

'...so I bought a few bits and pieces from the shop and found this place.' Mum always said 'bits and pieces' when she went shopping. She waved her arm in a sweeping gesture. 'Home sweet home,' she said.

'Are you going to keep looking for Dad's family?' Isla asked. In the grey light it was hard to make out Mum's face.

'Dunno. Can't think what to do, and it seems like no-one wants to help.'

Isla ran through the places they'd been, anything that could be a clue. They'd have to use all their cunning to evade capture. But she found it hard to think when her stomach felt like it had become a mouth and was eating itself from the inside.

'Is there any food left?' She buried her face into the contents of the orange plastic bag, pulled out a wrinkled apple and bit into its tough flesh.

'Surely we can find someone who wants to talk to us?' Isla said, spitting out bits of apple as she talked.

'I don't know, babs. I've tried.' Her words fell and returned with a faint echo from the dull stone walls. Isla realised the background noise of the helicopter was missing.

She took a last bite of apple and gave the rest to Lac. He gnawed at it with his gappy teeth. 'Can't eat it.' Mum bit off a large chunk for him to chew in the side of his mouth.

'I did mention to Mrs MacDonald that I knew someone who came from here. She said most of the young ones left the island and never came back. When I asked if she remembered Sandy MacLean, she told me, "He left here at 18. His dad was lost at sea some years back." That was all she said.'

'You what?' Isla's chin jutted out and her mouth gaped. 'You found someone who knew Dad?' Isla wanted to shake her. Why was Mum so difficult?

'Could have been him. But there's so many MacLeans.'

'There's lots of them in the graveyard.' Lac licked his fingers and tucked them into his sleeves. Luke Skywalker poked out of his waistband.

'But they're all dead. Don't you think it's weird, Mum, that there were so many people with our name?'

'I don't think Mrs MacDonald liked me.'

'So what? She's got to tell us where his family are!' Isla's screech bounced off the walls. 'Mum! It's a clue! We've got to follow it up. Take us back to Mrs MacDonald's house.'

Lac leapt to the door and pulled it open. Outside, a white haze blocked out everything beyond the bracken. 'Wow! Look at this!' Deep fog blanketed their world. His tone changed. 'Can't see a thing. How are we gonna find our way in this?'

Mum's eyes and mouth drooped. She shrugged.

Isla buried her face in her hands. Through her fingers, she said, 'We've got to try.'

CHAPTER 33

FOG

Archie didn't know what to do. Sitting on his grannie's coffee table, legs splayed apart, he looked at a newsflash on his phone from the island's WhatsApp group:

> *'Police are urgently looking for two children believed to be on the island of Mora after running away from their home in Birmingham. Their mother is also missing. A full-scale search is underway. Please report any sightings immediately.'*

Earlier, he'd heard a helicopter but now all he saw through the window was thick fog, blanking out his view. His grannie scrunched newspaper and laid it in the fire grate, the arms of her green fleece pushed up to the elbows. She threw a ball of paper into the middle of the room, and a ginger cat leapt off an armchair to pounce on it.

'I'll just get this fire laid, then I'll start on breakfast,' she said. She added a peat brick from the pile next to the fireplace. She looked outside at the whiteout the fog had caused. 'Gosh, see how the haar's come in. You couldn't see your hand in front of your face out there.'

'Listen, Gran.' Archie read out the message. 'It's those kids who I saw in the shop. Totally absolutely, it's them. And I met them out on the road the next day, too.' He didn't mention he'd given them a lift, or the joke he'd played on them.

Grannie sat back on her knees. 'More English people causing trouble,' she said.

'Gran!'

'Okay, I know. Poor bairns if they're lost.' She wiped her hands on a cloth. 'I heard about them a day or two ago. Mind you, they seem to be giving our islanders the run-around. Annie rang yesterday and told me she had them at her house for a while, but they gave her and Hector the slip.' She chuckled to herself. 'Nosy busybodies, Annie and Hector, always wanting to meddle and be the ones in the know. They must be furious.'

'Are you not worried about the kids, Grannie?'

The old woman held out a hand and Archie helped her up.

'I am,' she said. 'Especially if they were out all night. And now with the haar rolling in from the sea....' She spread her arms wide, the baggy fleece flopping over her small body '...there's some dangerous crags on the island.'

'And this bit: "*Their mother is also missing.*" Their ma was in the shop the day before. I swear it was her,' Archie said.

'Are you sure?'

'Hundred per cent. They talked the same way, you know, like *Peaky Blinders* on TV.'

'*Peaky Blinders*?'

Archie mimicked, 'You know, "*Oi* put a bullet in his head *yester-die*".'

Grannie looked like he'd gone mad.

'Brummies, Gran. That's how they talk.'

'That lady who was staying with Ella MacDonald? You say she's skipped off as well? Dear, dear.'

In the silence, the ginger cat rolled onto its back and stuck out a pink tongue to wash its tummy. Grannie walked through to the kitchen. 'Now for that breakfast.' Archie heard the fridge door suck open and the frying pan clatter onto the stove.

When he was a kid, Archie and his friends used to explore the land at this end of the island, beating through bracken, pretending they were smugglers bringing whisky from the mainland and hiding their contraband from the excise-men. He wouldn't be surprised if those wily kids had found the old bothy up above Smugglers Cove. It was a great hiding place.

He bent down to stroke the cat. He stood up again and shouted through to the kitchen.

'I'm going out in the tractor. With the haar coming down, the 'copter can't search for them. I've an idea where they might be.'

'You're going out before your breakfast? You can't see a thing out there. And I've got a fry on the go.'

Archie was at the door, pulling on his wellies. 'Later, Gran. Don't worry, I'll drive slowly.'

He jammed a beanie on his head, shouted 'Bye', and slammed the front door behind him. The gate clicked, the tractor spluttered into life, and Archie bounced away, red hair flying behind him.

He'd been driving a tractor since he was twelve and had known these lanes all his life. He swung off the road and bumped along an overgrown track. At the end, he stopped the engine and jumped off the tractor. Brushing aside fronds of chest-high bracken, he strode along the familiar path. His grannie said this had once been grazing land and the crofters took it in turns to stay at the bothy and mind the sheep. At shearing time, the hut was crammed with sweaty, sleeping bodies every night. 'Phew, the stink!' thought Archie, wiping misty dew from his forehead with his sleeve. All that way of life was gone now, the bothy left to children's imaginations, his Grannie had said.

He caught sight of the stone chimney. Moments later, he emerged from the bracken. Long grass was trodden down outside the bothy, and the front door stood ajar. Archie shoved it open and bent forward to look inside. It was empty. He stepped in, and stood in the middle of the room, hands on hips and elbows sticking outward. He'd been sure he'd find them.

He kicked a water bottle and lifted the edge of a blanket. An orange plastic bag full of apple cores and food packaging lay discarded in a corner.

'Now what?' he said to the abandoned space. He stood at the door and screwed up his face to peer through the mist.

Outside, three pairs of eyes peeked through the bracken and watched the boy re-appear, carrying the bag of rubbish and ducking his head through the low doorway. The three heads swivelled, eyes following his steps until he entered the path. They didn't stop watching until his red hair disappeared into the fog.

The trio emerged from their hiding place, brushing drops of moisture from their arms. Apart from the faint chug-chug of a tractor engine, they couldn't hear anything. Not the roar of the sea, no seagull calls, no rushing wind. Just their own hearts hammering in their chests.

'Nearly caught.' Isla's hair was damp. She checked her zinger, making double sure she'd hooked it properly behind her ear with the tip positioned right inside.

Mum held Isla and Lac to her, one each side. 'All I need is a pair of wings for you to hide under, and I'd be a fully-fledged mother hen.' They approached the hut.

'Right,' she said. 'We're going to get out of here. We're not welcome, we'd be better off back home.'

Home. What a weird word. Isla considered the damp, hazy world around her: unkempt ferns, a broken-down hut, grass slippery with dew, an unfamiliar mountain looming behind them, and the ever-present sea which she knew was there even though she could neither see nor hear it.

Mum went inside and bundled up the blankets, and Lac dragged her holdall from its hiding place in the bracken. Isla held it open, while Mum and Lac stowed the blankets inside.

'Thought so,' a deep voice said. Isla jumped. Lac and Mum froze.

CHAPTER 34

FOUND

Archie straightened up from his bent stance and marched forward from the path's entrance.

'You!' Isla said.

'Aye, me.'

Isla's heart sank. Blinking away drops of moisture dribbling into her eyes, she said, 'Mum, it's that horrible boy I was telling you about.'

Mum looked at Archie, then at the gap in the bracken he'd come from.

'But…..' Mum pointed down the path towards the tractor, thrumming out of sight.

Archie grinned. 'Left the engine running. I guessed you might still be here.'

'How?' Lac asked.

Archie tapped his nose. 'I wasn't a boy scout for nothing. So this is your ma?' He turned to face her. 'Hello there, I work in the shop.'

Mum's mouth was a gaping hole. She didn't speak.

'I've come to help you,' he said.

Isla couldn't help tears running down her cheeks. 'Don't trust him, Mum. That's what he said last time. He sent us the wrong way, that wasn't helping.'

'Sorry about that.'

'Sorry?'

'It was a bit of fun. Two kids on an adventure, straight out of the films – *Home Alone* in reverse.'

This boy was so annoying. Isla punched the air. 'If you mess us around again, I'll kill you.'

'Isla!' Mum held her arm.

A telling-off from Mum was the last thing she needed. 'Honest, Mum, he caused us so much trouble. It's his fault I was locked up and you had to rescue me.' She strained against Mum's hand holding her. 'Let me get at him, the dirty rat.'

Archie laughed out loud and held out his open palms in front of him. 'Whoa, hey, don't be like that. Really, I'm sorry.' He formed a V-shaped peace sign with two fingers. 'Pax, okay?' He walked closer. 'Nobody wants to hurt you. Look, you've found your ma, that's great. Why don't you come with me to my grannie's? She's cooking a fry for breakfast.'

'Fry what?' Lac asked, looking up into the boy's face.

'Bacon, sausages, eggs at least, I reckon.'

Lac jiggled up and down. 'Mum, we've got to go. Pleeeeease.'

'She'll be glad to have you, so she will. And she'll be happy to tell Annie and Hector she has them at her house.' Archie grinned.

'Who?' Mum's grip tightened on Isla's wrist.

'The couple at the end of the road where all the wild raspberries grow.'

'No, don't tell anyone,' Mum said.

'Ok, ok. Come on, let's get out of the wet.' Archie turned. 'And get some food in our bellies.'

They didn't need any further invitation.

'All in?' Archie shouted. Squashed together on two seats, they bumped along through the hazy, muffled world, the fog obscuring their view on all sides. Archie wasn't bothered, he knew all the bumps and potholes to avoid. After a few minutes, he swerved from the road onto a patch of grass and switched off the engine. 'Here it is.'

Behind a wall sat a low cottage surrounded by grass. They jumped off the tractor and followed Archie through stone gateposts as tall as Lac, and up a path where giant sunflowers nodded down at them like their back garden in Birmingham. Isla shook her head to clear away jumbled thoughts of home. That was the life she'd left behind. This was her life now.

As she stared at a horseshoe door-knocker in front of them, the door yawned open. An old woman wearing a faded green fleece looked at them and then at her grandson.

'Archie?'

'You'll never guess what, Grannie. Here's some visitors for your famous breakfast scran.'

The old lady shifted her gaze to the children and wrinkled her nose. Wisps of hair that had escaped from her pony-tail waved gently in the breeze.

'You found them?' she asked, looking Isla and Lac up and down and then turning her gaze to Mum. Isla opened her mouth to say hello, but it was so dry, all that came out was, 'Uh.' She tried to smile instead through cracked lips.

Oh no, she could feel hiccups starting. Quietly jerking, she tried to suppress them.

'Yes, Grannie, in the bothy by Smugglers Cove. These are the kids who've been missing all week. They were out in that storm we had on Thursday.'

'Surely not. It was a terrible night.' She pushed the stray strand of hair behind her ear. 'And you're their mammy?'

Mum didn't answer.

'Can't they speak?' the old lady asked.

'Hel– hic– hell– hic–' Isla was trying her hardest to say hello.

'Oh dear, you need a drink of water. But look at the state of you.' Grannie stepped forward and cast her eyes over Isla's clothes. 'And the little one.'

Mum shifted her feet. 'We won't stay if we're not wanted.'

'Don't be like that, lovey. Come on in.' The old woman stood back to let them into her home. 'Fáilte.'

'That means welcome,' Archie said.

CHAPTER 35

FRY

The old woman led them through a dark hallway and opened the door to a small living room. In the corner, a ginger cat slept curled up in a basket. As the old woman stood aside, Isla caught sight of her scruffy face in a mirror on the wall, above a flickering fire.

Staring back at her was a girl with wild hair, a red nose and smudges down her cheeks. A beam of light flashed off Mum's glasses. Although this felt like a dream, she knew she was actually here for real. Dirt coated her jeans, torn at the knees, and a white rim on the denim above the ankle had been left by the sea when she'd tried to calm her stinging foot. Blood-crusted scabs poked out of her ripped trousers. She held out her hands, which were covered in bites and scratches.

'The wee midgies have eaten them to bits,' the old woman said to the cat. She turned to Mum. 'Sit down, dear. Let's get you a cup of tea. Archie, the kettle's not long boiled.'

Mum just stood in the middle of the room. Isla felt like the fog had filled her head. She held her breath, but the hiccups still jogged her chest.

The old woman touched Isla's sleeve. 'And some water for this one,' she called to Archie in the kitchen. She looked Isla up and down. 'You are in a sorry state, aren't you?' Isla hic-sniffed.

The baggy fleece draped the old woman's knees as she bent down to Lac. 'Are you hungry?' she asked in a gentle voice.

Lac's shaggy red hair flopped up and down with his nodding head.

'Of course you are. Come on, let's fix that.' She took Lac's hand, and they went through a low doorway. Mum followed, and Isla trailed after them into the kitchen.

'I've been staying at Mrs MacDonald's,' Mum said.

'Yes, I know.' The old woman pulled out a chair for Lac to sit at the table. 'Help yourself to bread and butter while I cook up the bacon and eggs.'

'Is there sausages?'

Archie opened the fridge and took out two packets of square slices.

'This is our sort of sausage,' he said. 'And tattie scones – will you do them too, Grannie?'

'Look, Mum, square sausages.'

Mum sat next to Lac. She spread butter on two pieces of bread and handed one to him while Archie put a blue striped mug of steaming tea in front of her.

'I was hoping to find out about my husband.'

Isla wished Mum wouldn't mumble.

The old woman opened a pile of bacon wrapped in paper and each slice sputtered as she laid them in the frying pan on the cooker. 'What's that, dear?'

'He told me he came from this island,' she said to the woman's back.

Isla stood by the door glugging water. The bacon smell was unbelievable.

The grannie twisted round from the stove and beckoned to her. 'Come and sit over here, hen. Better wash your hands first. And you,' she tapped Lac's shoulder. Filth ran off their palms as they soaped and rinsed them under the tap before attacking the mountain of bread that Mum had buttered.

Turning the bacon with a fork, the grannie asked Mum over her shoulder, 'Who's that you were talking about?'

'My husband, the children's father. I haven't seen him for seven years.'

Ask her, Mum. She's bound to know something.

'He was from Mora, you say?' Fantastic frying smells were filling the kitchen as the old woman flipped the squares of sausage and cracked an egg into the pan.

Isla clenched her fists under the table. *Say yes, tell her everything you know. We might not get another chance.*

Isla's zinger tinkled with high-pitched clinking of knives and forks when Archie rummaged in the cutlery drawer. Hot fat sizzled as the grannie dropped more eggs in the pan.

'He left suddenly when the children were small.' Mum wiped crumbs from Lac's mouth.

'I was only a baby,' he said, starting on another piece of bread, 'and Isla was five.'

Isla silently willed Mum to go on. *Don't clam up now, pleeeease.* She tried to imagine how Hermione Granger would pull the question out of Mum's mouth.

'Sandy MacLean – did you know him?' Mum asked.

Isla felt sick. Lac stopped chewing, a crust sticking out of his mouth.

Sizzle, went the eggs.

The woman laughed out loud. 'Ha, same name as my son.' She turned to face Mum and put her hands on her hips. 'But he never married. I'm not sure your ex was telling the truth. Could have been any of the islands, we have plenty of them. There are enough MacLeans to fill a fleet of buses, and half the men are called Sandy.'

'Short for Alexander?' Isla asked.

'Aye.'

'He definitely said Mora,' Mum said, blowing into her cup of tea.

'Sometimes he was called Mac,' Isla said.

'That's what they get called in England.' The grannie shook the frying pan. 'Sounds like he was having you on. I know all the MacLeans on this island going back for a hundred years. It was my husband's family; I was a MacDonald by birth.'

The woman put two plates stacked with eggs, bacon, potato cake and a sausage patty in front of Isla and Lac. 'Get your teeth round that, both of you.' She leaned over and put her hand over Mum's. 'I'm sorry, lovey, your husband has lied to you. Ooh, your hands are cold. Drink your tea.'

Archie was fiddling with something on a pedestal that he'd picked up from a shelf. 'Put that down, Archie, come and have your breakfast,' Grannie said.

'I know he lied. At first, he told me his name was Andy McCluskey,' Mum said.

'Definitely not. The only Andy McCluskey from Mora passed away when he was six years old, poor little mite. Leukaemia. His ma never got over it.' She looked up at the ceiling. 'Gus am bris an là.'

'What does that mean?' Lac asked.

Archie butted in. 'Until the day breaks. Our way of saying Rest in Peace.' He stood the silver object on the table. It was a little cross with a circle, the same as in the graveyard. Isla swallowed hard. The same as the ring on her thumb.

Mum was still white as a sheet.

'All right dearie? Have some of this, you'll feel better after you've eaten.' She put a full plate in front of Mum.

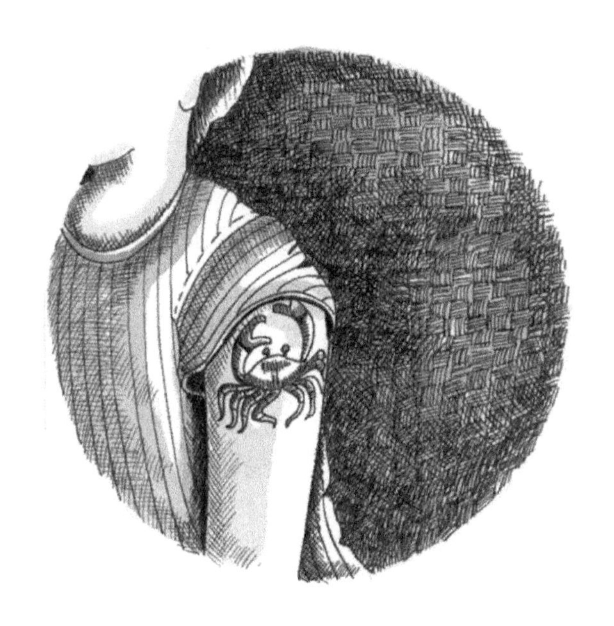

CHAPTER 36

TATTOO

'Come on,' Archie said to Isla. 'Let's take this toast and have a chat. If you trust me now.' His grin was friendly, not mocking, and Isla managed to smile back.

In the living room, he placed the silver cross on the mantelpiece above the fire, next to an old-fashioned clock. As he stretched out on the settee, the cat jumped onto his tummy and started purring. Its fur was a softer, lighter ginger than Archie's hair.

'Can I ask you something?' One hand rammed toast into his mouth, the other scratched the cat behind its ears.

Isla nodded, relaxing back into a comfy armchair.

He pointed to her right ear. 'Why do you call that thing a zinger?'

Isla smiled. 'When I was little, I called it an ear-singer, but it was easier to say zinger.'

'That's really cool.' He sat up, picked up the cat in his big hands, and placed it, still curled up, onto the cushion next to him. He shrugged off his sweatshirt. 'It's always so hot at my gran's.' Underneath, a green vest pronounced *Fowl Youth*. 'That's my band.'

But Isla's eyes were fixed on the tattoo on his shoulder. A red crab.

He screwed his head round to look at it and stroked the image with two fingers. 'Do you like it? A lady on the island does this design.'

'My dad had a tattoo of a crab like that.' Isla had been scared of its pincers. 'How come you've got the same one?'

'It's an island thing, lots of guys do it. My uncle's got one, and as soon as I was sixteen, I got my own.'

'I thought you had to be eighteen.'

He flexed his arm muscles. 'We do things differently up here.'

Isla gripped the soft arms of her chair. She couldn't understand what he meant; he was talking in riddles again. 'I can't work this out. Everybody on this island seems to be connected to everyone else.'

He crossed his arms behind his head, exposing hairy armpits. Ginger, like his hair. 'Well, I'm Archie MacKinnon. In the holidays I work in the shop, but I go to school on the mainland, like all the kids do.' He jerked his head towards the kitchen. 'That's my gran in there. My ma – she's not my real ma because I'm adopted – but like I was saying, my ma is sister to Uncle Sandy, but I never saw him when I was little. He went away to join the polis in England.'

Isla blinked. The last bite of toast hurt her throat as she gulped it down. She scratched her head and rubbed her thigh. She was definitely awake. Hugging her body tightly with shoulders hunched, eyebrows drawn together, Isla stared into the orange flames of the fire.

'Dad didn't have a sister.'

'I mean, she *is* my real ma, it's not like she's fake, but she's not my birth mother.'

The cat twitched in its sleep, in the middle of a dream. Isla glanced at the clock: twenty past one. Was that all? She'd lost track of ordinary things like times of day and meal-times. *Fake identity* and *fake parents* swirled around in her mind.

Archie leant sideways on his elbow, and the cat jumped off and tiptoed to its basket in the corner by the fire. 'Your da must be a different Sandy MacLean. Like Grannie said, there's plenty of 'em. Definitely not my uncle Sandy who was in the polis.'

'No chance, He was against the police. They arrested him for being a protester.'

Archie passed his hand over the top of his head. 'Wow. Awesome. What was he protesting?'

'Him and my mum. They were climate activists. They were really into it. Lots of protests. I went with them once when I was little.' Isla was beginning to like Archie; he was easy to talk to now that they weren't having to deal with difficult stuff.

'Cool.' Archie lay down again.

'My dad was hiding from the police.'

His head bobbed up on its long neck. 'Never!'

'He was.' Isla felt proud. 'He was trying to save the planet, and the police were going to arrest him again.' She wasn't sure if she was making some of this up.

Then he spoke in an exaggerated whisper, as if there was a secret between them.

'Imagine my Uncle Sandy arresting your dadaigh and asking his name. Wouldn't that be funny?' His ideas seemed to be taking shape, and he sounded like a TV detective. He sat up, knees splayed apart, face eager with the story. But his brow furrowed. 'Nah. When Uncle Sandy came back – '

'Back?'

'– my grannie said he was different.'

'Is that what you meant by doing things differently on the islands?'

'No, he had a terrible sadness. He wouldn't talk to my ma or anyone. Even my gran didn't know what it was.'

In the fireplace, the pyramid of half-burnt blocks hissed and crumpled, exposing white-hot ashy undersides.

The opening door broke the silence. Lac plumped himself on the settee next to Archie, and Mum placed a bowl of biscuits on the coffee table. The old woman brought a stack of plates. Her lips were pressed together, and her eyes were red.

'Sit down, dearies. Move over, Archie. This wee lad says his name is Lachlan. Lachlan MacLean, that was my husband's name.' She set the plates down on the table. 'My Lachlan was lost at sea six long years ago.'

Was she crying? She sounded so sad. Isla and Lachlan looked at each other and mouthed: 'Lost at sea.'

'Strange to have a boy here with his name. Where did you say you were from, my dear?'

'Birmingham.'

'Oh yes, away down in England. My boy Sandy was over the water for many years.'

Before sitting in the armchair beside the fire, she turned on a standard lamp which cast a glow into the room. 'The haar's slipping away, but I still think we need a bit more light in here.'

'Haar?' Mum asked.

'Fog,' Archie said from the other end of the settee.

It might be clearer outside, but Isla's brain was still totally fogged up. Despite feeling stuffed, she took a biscuit. Lac held one in each hand. The old woman jiggled the glowing embers with a black metal poker.

'Birmingham.' She looked at Isla in the armchair and Lac on the settee. 'But you must have Scots parents, to have names like Isla and Lachlan.'

'My husband was Scottish, he suggested their names,' Mum said. Lac climbed onto Mum's lap, and she tossed back her hair and put both arms round him, resting her chin on top of his head.

'Oh yes, your husband Sandy.' She added a brick of peat to the grate.

The cat stood up, stretched, and stepped out of its basket. It placed one white-tipped foot in front of the other like a dancer, walked over to the armchair, jumped up and nudged Grannie's arm with its head.

The woman looked at Isla's hand. 'Let me see that ring.'

Isla pulled it off her thumb and handed it over. The grannie held it up to the light, examining some scratches on the inside. She looked at Mum.

'I thought so, from what you were saying in the kitchen. It's the one, right enough.'

CHAPTER 37

DISCOVERED

Before anyone could ask what the old woman meant, a mechanical sound filled the air.

WHUPPA-WHUPPA-WHUPPA.

Archie stood up and loped to the window. 'The fog's cleared.' He craned his neck. 'The helicopter is up over the north end. I reckon it's flying over the lake just now.' He turned round and grinned. 'Maybe it's looking for floating bodies.' He blew out his cheeks and made a bloated dead-face. Isla glared at him – she couldn't believe he was making a joke.

'Archie,' Grannie said, 'that's not funny.'

'Sorry, Grannie.' He checked his phone and read out:

'The search for the missing children has narrowed to the north of the island. It is believed they spent the night in the old bothy near Smugglers Cove.'

What? How did they know that? Isla looked at Archie. He's seventeen. Does that mean he's on the adults' side. Is Archie a traitor?

Lac wriggled off Mum's knee and climbed up onto the deep windowsill. The whirring noise was getting louder.

'It's heading this way. We're gonna be rescued,' he yelled. He leapt off the sill and disappeared through the door, ran out the front door, tore past the sunflowers and through the head-high gateposts.

'Come back, it's dangerous!' Mum screamed. She dashed after him.

Archie belted past her. Lac jumped up and down, waving and shouting on the stretch of grass outside the gate. The helicopter flew overhead then wheeled round in response to Lac's frenzied waving and circled above them.

'STAND BACK' boomed an amplified voice.

Archie lunged for Lac, pulling him out of the way. Mum grabbed Lac's wrist and hugged him to her. Isla took her arm on the other side. They all stood by Grannie's stone wall, faces lifted upwards, as the helicopter hovered above them, the wind from its rotors flattening the grass. Three thick orange v-shaped stripes – called chevrons, thought Isla – were painted on its underside, next to COASTGUARD RESCUE in black letters. The downdraft tore at their clothes, and Archie's hair looked like it was going to take off, beanie and all. The deafening noise turned the scene into a silent movie.

As it descended, back tail wobbling three metres from the ground and flashing an orange landing light, the rotors slowed.

The blurred whirling disc above the helicopter turned into five distinct blades and the WHUPPA-WHUPPA noise acquired a whine and then a swish-swish-swish of individual blades, each shaped like an oar, whipping though the air.

A rapturous smile lit up Lac's face, watching the machine judder gently from side to side and land with a small bump. The pilot shut off the engine, the tail rotor came to a stop, and the overhead blades rotated gracefully.

For a few moments, nothing moved except the still turning rotors, and up above, three seagulls circling and soaring in graceful arcs. An orange boiler-suited figure stood framed in the helicopter's door. He placed his foot onto the boarding step, jumped down and stood for a moment under the blades turning slowly above his head. As he walked beyond their orbit he raised his visor, undid the chin clasp of his yellow helmet and eased it off his head. Red hair sprang out and his hand smoothed a ginger beard.

Isla felt Mum's body go rigid. The rotor blades stopped turning, leaving her ears ringing. Instead of calm, a tension fizzed through Mum like electricity.

Up above, a sudden squawk lifted her attention to a fight between a seagull and a brown bird. She should be used to it by now.

Archie was distracted by the airborne scrap too. 'Typical bonxie,' he said, 'always stealing from the gulls.' Incomprehensible yet again. What on earth was a bonxie? Another orange-clad figure stepped down onto the grass and shook out long hair as she removed her helmet.

Isla screwed her eyes shut then shook her head before opening them again. The pilot in front of them was standing against bright light, making his outline hazy.

'Sandy?' Mum squeaked.

Isla whipped her head towards Mum, and then back to the pilot.

Lac stepped forward, hands over his ears, staring at the orange suit, the man with the rust-coloured hair, same as him. Archie stood beside him, rusty-red hair flowing from his beanie hat.

The old woman spoke first.

'Hello, son. Here's the children you've been out looking for.'

'Hello, Ma,' the pilot said, staring at Isla, Lac and Mum.

In the air above them, reinforcements joined the embattled seagull, outnumbering the brown bird by six to one. The whole crowd of them flew out over the sea. A whiff of seaweed reminded Isla how close they were to the sea's edge.

'Is it really you?' Mum asked.

Quiet filled the air.

The pilot's mouth fell open and thick veins stood out on the stalk of his neck. 'So it is you.' *Yoo.*

That voice swam up from Isla's memory. She felt like her life was entangled like fronds of drifting seaweed, stranded by the tide and then floating off again in a jumbled mass.

'It's my uncle Sandy,' Archie told Lac, flicking his hair back.

An ice-cold shiver chilled Isla all over. Her voice shook. 'Da-ad?' she whispered, hands either side of her face.

The pilot looked from Mum to Isla and back again.

'Why are you here?' Mum said through clenched teeth. 'What are you doing?' Her fists were bunched by her sides, as if she might punch him.

Wind whistled in rocks at the shore.

Lac stepped forward. He planted his feet wide and looked up at the apparition. 'Are you real? What's your name?'

'Sandy MacLean.'

Isla was frozen to the spot, speechless.

'I'm Lachlan MacLean.'

He put his helmet on the ground and knelt down.

'You're Lachlan MacLean?'

Lac nodded. 'But everyone calls me Lac.' He stretched out a finger and poked the chest of the pilot's overalls. 'Are you a ghost?' When there was no response, he shouted into his face: 'ARE YOU A GHOST? You're dead. You should be bleeding. Ghosts who died in a crash have injuries.'

He kicked the pilot's leg as hard as he could. 'You're not dead. You're real. You should be dead.'

'Hey, hey! Hold it little feller.' The pilot held Lac's shoulders at arm's length so he couldn't aim any more kicks.

'GET YOUR HANDS OFF HIM!' screamed Mum, leaping forward and pulling Lac towards her, encircling him with her arms.

The pilot stood up, still looking at Lac. 'Why should I be dead?'

'Your motorbike!' Lac shouted across the space between them.

'I never had a motorbike. I had a van.'

Lac burst into tears. 'You're not our dad then.' He slipped out of Mum's grasp and collapsed onto his knees, buried his head in his arms and howled. The high-pitched weeping penetrated Isla's zinger.

'Mum, is it Dad or not?' Isla asked above the noise.

Looking through the fingers covering her face, Mum nodded.

A crack in Isla's sore lips split open painfully. Her mouth was so dry she couldn't swallow. She felt like rubbing salt into the wound so that the pain would overwhelm this moment. She couldn't bear to think that this – that – man, that stranger – was him who she'd been writing letters to, who she'd imagined in her head all these years, nothing like this figure in front of her.

'Sandy, do you mind telling me what's going on?' the old woman said.

He stood like a statue, but his eyes flicked between all the people outside the cottage.

Mum didn't give him a chance to reply. 'I can't believe it. You left us. Can you imagine what that felt like? Never knowing where you were, or even who you were. Or if you were still alive. You must have hated us, to just walk out like that. Seven years in limbo. Feeling hated, worthless.'

This was so weird. In the last few days, Isla kept hearing the same thing. Limbo. Disappeared. She couldn't imagine how Hermione would deal with a situation like this. Her parents never hated each other and always stuck together.

The pilot stepped towards Mum.

'Don't come near me,' she said in an icy voice.

He looked like he'd been slapped in the face, but squared his shoulders again and shifted his gaze.

'Isla?'

She gulped when he said her name.

'Leave her alone!' Mum screamed.

The grannie touched Mum's sleeve. 'Now, now dear. There's no cause for skriking like that.' Mum shook her off and turned away.

Isla lost it. She yelled at the top of her voice. 'Mum – stop it. You came all this way to find out about him, and he is HERE.'

'Like a mirage,' Mum said, as if he was going to disappear into thin air any second.

Lac uncurled from his grief-stricken position. Confusion filled his tear-stained face. 'What's a mirage?' No-one answered.

The pilot jammed the helmet back on his head, turned and walked towards the helicopter. He spoke to his co-pilot in the orange suit, *Flora Stewart* displayed on her name badge. 'Sorry, Flora, I can't deal with this. You'll have to take over.'

Isla screeched at him, 'No! Come back. You can't leave us again!' She leapt forward, grabbed his elbow and turned him around roughly. 'Dad!'

The co-pilot moved to join him, but Lac stumbled across the grass and pushed her in the stomach. 'Get away from my sister,' he declared. Flora staggered in surprise, and she stopped mid-stride.

The pilot's visor masked his face, making him look like an alien invader. Isla saw trembling lips in the middle of his beard. A sensation flowed up from her feet and through her body. She felt strong. It wasn't just up to Mum to sort everything out.

She hadn't noticed the grannie taking Mum's hand in both of hers but she heard the hard-edged voice addressing the man. 'Answer me, son. Are these bairns your children?'

The pilot flinched. He took his helmet off again. His beard was wet with tears. He nodded.

The grannie made a funny noise, half-growl half-bray like a donkey. 'You'd better come inside and explain yourself properly.' She led the way, followed by her son and Isla's mum.

Isla didn't know what to do. Should she go with the grown-ups? Before she could decide, Archie put his arm around her shoulder.

'This is amazing. We must be cousins,' he said.

CHAPTER 38

CONFUSION AND LIES

Lac followed the co-pilot, who was standing outside the helicopter's open door. She spoke into a handset at the end of a curly wire.

'Echo Two to Mora coastguard: Search operation complete. Children found. Repeat: Children found, safe and unhurt. Location: Balevulin, the MacLean house. Inform polis. Returning to base at fifteen hundred hours. All stand down. Over.'

A reply came over the radio loud and clear. 'Great job, Echo Two. Message received. Over and out.'

She replaced the handset and winked at Lac. He winked back. She beckoned him over and pointed inside the cabin. He poked his head inside, then looked back at Flora. When she nodded, he put his foot on the boarding step, reached for the handrails and pulled himself up. She climbed in, showed him into the cockpit and gestured for him to sit in the pilot's seat.

He bounced up and down and yelled, 'I'M IN THE PILOT'S SEAT!' He stretched his right hand round the joystick and gazed at a sea of luminous dials in front of him. His feet strained to reach the pedals, while Flora, in the co-pilot's chair, began to explain all the controls.

Outside the cottage, Isla felt like her feet were glued to the ground.

'Cousins?' she asked.

Archie leant on the gatepost, grinning. He didn't seem like a clever-dick anymore.

'I reckon my ma is your auntie.'

'Auntie?'

Isla's brain couldn't compute. She ran her fingers through her matted hair, wincing when they got stuck in a tangled knot and yanked her scalp.

'And my grannie in the house,' he jerked his head towards the front door, 'she's *our* grannie.'

'I can't believe it.'

'Me neither. Fancy Uncle Sandy never saying.'

'Our grannie.' Cousin. Auntie. Grannie. These words felt weird on Isla's tongue. Nice weird, like dipping into a packet of Haribo Zingfest – sour and tasty at the same time.

'Let's go inside,' Archie said.

'Wait, I need to get Lac.'

It was not easy getting him out of the helicopter.

'Isla, look at me,' he shouted over his shoulder. 'I'm flying the 'copter. This is the throttle – it can fly two hundred miles an hour! Flora's my co-pilot.'

'Sounds like you need to touch base with your family,' Flora said. 'You can come back later and have another go.'

'Really?'

'For sure. But off you go now, your sister's waiting for you.'

Lac backed out of the cockpit and lowered himself down to the ground. He took Isla's hand, and they joined Archie at the gate to the cottage. They pushed open the front door but stopped. Voices filtered through from the living room. Isla put her finger to her lips, and they all huddled close in the corridor.

'Your Sandy is my Sandy,' a voice the other side of the door said.

'That's Grannie,' Archie whispered.

'Shhh,' Isla hissed.

A deep voice came next, the one she knew from when she was small. That was full-on weird, hearing the strange-but-familiar tones.

'I never wanted to leave you.' A hesitation, then he continued. 'I was just going to hide away for a while. I was on a caution with my superior officer. My ma and pa took me in. I couldn't face what I'd done. If I didn't think about it – you – it was better.' Another silence. 'Life was bearable.'

'Bearable for you, maybe,' said Mum. Isla could picture her pinched lips and steely eyes. 'Not for us.'

'I couldn't come back,' he said. 'If I stayed here, everything was just in limbo. Even though I couldn't see you, you were still there. I was terrified of losing you forever.'

Limbo? Not again. Isla turned to her brother and cousin. 'He's lying.' She burst through the door into a wave of heat and planted her feet on the worn carpet. Sweat broke out under her armpits, but her clammy palms were cold.

'You weren't terrified of losing us. You were here all that time. You abandoned us.' That word felt just right.

Dad – did Isla dare to think of him like that? Dad was leaning on the dresser near the window and the light caught beads of sweat on his forehead. He was only a few paces away, but the gap between them seemed like a huge gulf.

Grannie said, 'He came home, I don't know why. But he helped my Lachlan with the animals and sometimes the two of them went out fishing at night. Often came back in the morning with a good haul of haddock in the boat, and usually a few crabs.'

The crab tattoo.

Isla saw Grannie looking out of the window with shimmering eyes. 'But my Lachlan was alone on the boat that night I lost him in a big storm.'

'There now, Ma,' Dad said, and turned towards Isla. 'After my pa died, I had to support my ma.'

Isla ground her teeth. 'Like we didn't exist? Some dad you are.' She turned her back on him and uttered a frustrated growl. Lac stood in the doorway, a mini-me of Archie behind him. With a shock, Isla realised how much they looked alike.

She spun on her heel and asked her new Grannie sitting in the armchair by the fire, 'How could you keep him from us?'

The clock ticked as if it was saying, *Spit it out,* a bit like a teacher tapping a pen on their finger, waiting for your pathetic excuse.

Grannie pinched her nose and sniffed. 'I didn't know. I knew something was wrong, but he wouldn't say what was the matter. I thought it was girl trouble that he didn't want to talk about. He was up here for a wee while, and when he left again, we presumed it was all sorted out. But two years later he was back. I never expected all this, though.' She waved her hand around the room. 'I hadn't any notion there was a wife and kiddies.'

Hearing the word 'kiddies', Lac dodged past Isla and crossed the room to sit next to Mum on the settee. He reached down the cushion behind him and pulled out Luke Skywalker.

'Luke wants to know why I'm called Lachlan.'

Now Mum's voice rang out loud.

'Yeah Sandy, what were you playing at? You called our son after your dad, and you never said?'

'I came back to you once,' Dad said. 'I couldn't bear to be separated from you and the kids.'

Liar. Isla was desperate to believe him, but she just couldn't.

Grannie rubbed her hands together. 'Awful cruel, to lose your husband in a fishing accident.' She shook her head. Isla thought she heard her whimper, but realised it was a lamb bleating outside.

'Lost at sea,' Lac muttered.

Mum said, in a flat voice, 'I lost my husband when you got your son back.'

A branch scratched at the window. The *skrrrk* sound scraped at Isla's brain.

Tick, tick, went the clock. *Get on with it.* That invisible beetle crawling up her spine had returned.

'What did you mean by "superior officer"?' she asked Dad. 'I never heard of campaigners having bosses. Greta Thunberg definitely hasn't.'

'Hang on,' Archie said, 'I thought you were a polis.'

'That's right, a polis,' echoed Grannie.

'No, no.' Isla shook her head. 'They were climate protesters, isn't that right, Mum?' She was boiling hot and felt a bit sick.

'Yep,' Mum said, throwing her head back so her glasses glinted in the firelight. 'Me and Mac – Sandy – , both of us. Only Mac….'

She sat up straight. Lac stood up on the settee, dirty shoes on the cushions.

Dad looked like he'd swallowed a dead fish. His face was grey and the lump of his Adam's apple quivered in his throat.

Skrrrk went the branch.

CHAPTER 39

TRUTH AT LAST

Pink splodges appeared on Grannie's cheeks, and she blinked a few times. 'It's so hot in here.'

She levered herself out of the armchair and opened the door to the kitchen. She beckoned, 'Give me a wee hand, son.' Dad followed her like a robot, one foot in front of another, arms dangling by his sides.

When they had gone, Isla asked, 'Did you know Dad had run away here, Mum?'

'No.'

'Do you mean it?'

'Honest.'

'But you lied too. You told us he was dead.' Isla felt like she was going to puke, she had to get out of there. Tears sprang from her eyes, making everything blurry as she blundered through the front door and out of the gate. She flung herself facedown onto wet grass, disturbing a bird that flew away crying *oo-weee*.

She heard Mum calling. 'Isla, darling.' A hand on her back. 'Don't be like that, babs.'

'Why not? I hate my life. I hate Dad. And you,' she added, although that last bit wasn't really true. She spoke into a dark space where the grass tickled her lips. 'I always had this sneaking feeling that Dad wasn't dead. I told myself I was stupid. I thought there was something wrong with me for believing he was still alive. For writing him letters.'

'Letters?'

'Secret letters.' She lifted her head and turned her tear-stained face to Mum. 'Now I find out he was a policeman, but not a normal one, because police officers are honest, but Dad lied. He lied to his own family.' Bits of grass stuck to her cheeks. 'And you knew.' A fresh bout of crying took over, alongside the dreaded hiccups.

'Babs, we'll be okay, we've got each other.'

Painful *hic*. Isla wished she could believe Mum, but she just couldn't. 'There's something you're not telling us, isn't there?' She sat up. O*o-weee* called the bird from a safe distance, sounding like it wanted its patch of grass back.

Mum, kneeling beside her, swallowed, as if a pill was stuck halfway down her throat. 'When I met your dad, he was an undercover cop, but I didn't know,' she said in a rush, her face flushing deep red.

Isla's heart did a double beat.

'What?' A rush of disjointed words flooded her brain. Mum's email: Intelligence operation. Google: undercover. From the caravan window: *Fake campaigners.* 'I heard about this. Protesters who were really police officers.' She curled her fingers into fists. 'But he can't have been one of them. He was on the run from the police.'

Mum shook her head. 'He made that up. He *was* the police.'

Isla was gobsmacked. That woman on the news: *He deceived me. He was a trained liar.*

'You didn't know?' She managed to swallow a hiccup.

'Not until he told me, before he left the second time.' She took a breath. 'And...'

'And?'

'... and confessed.'

O*o-weee.* Isla watched the green and white bird with a strange tuft on its head running back and forth on the grass, calling constantly, *oo-weee oo-weee.*

Mum blinked several times. 'Mac told me it was a deadly secret. It was called "deep cover". He was told - ordered - to join the protest movement.' She screwed her fists into her eyes, rubbing hard as if she could erase the images. 'Getting involved meant getting a girlfriend - me. It was his job,' Mum said. 'I was his job,' she repeated, looking as if she'd just bitten into an apple full of maggots. 'He pretended to care about the planet but all the time he was really a policeman, reporting on us activists.'

Isla recalled that woman she'd heard on TV when she was locked in the old couple's bathroom.

'My husband had a van, and used to offer people lifts after meetings, so he could find out where they lived.'

'You really didn't know?'

She shook her head. 'To me he was Mac, my boyfriend. Your father. Turns out I married a stranger.'

Nameless stranger, that TV woman had said. *Oo-weee oo-weee,* the bird wailed.

'Andy McCluskey,' Isla said. *Fake identity.*

Mum pushed her mass of hair off her face. 'How did you know?'

'I'm not daft. You mentioned it once by mistake, and then in the graveyard, that little grave upset you so much.'

Mum sat back, hugging her knees. 'I had no idea. I married Andy McCluskey, but then found out he was really Sandy MacLean.'

'Did Aunty Lou know?' Isla asked.

Mum shook her head. She leant forward and put her head in her hands. 'I couldn't tell anyone. I felt stupid, lost.'

'And then…..' Isla knew what came next. *Pretended he'd died.*

The bird had gone quiet, and a fine mist of rain had begun to fall. Tiny droplets clung to Mum's glasses. Isla felt like the tables were turned, it was up to her now to comfort Mum. The hiccups had gone. She stood up.

'We'd better go in. We're soaking wet.'

'Don't think I can face him.' But Mum scrambled onto her feet and trailed behind Isla along the path, past the sunflowers buzzing with bees which echoed a furious buzzing inside Isla's head. The bees didn't seem to mind the drizzle.

There was no sign of Dad or Grannie in the living room. Lac jumped on Mum. 'Where've you *beeeen*? Archie and me have been playing "Guess who?" It's his turn now.' He held on, legs round Mum's middle. She lifted him down.

Isla noticed the cat, curled up in its basket, and was angry that it had a warm and cosy life, with no worries or problems, just eat and sleep and be stroked.

'I've got something to tell you about your dad,' Mum said.

'What? He's in there.' Lac's thumb pointed towards the kitchen door. He flumped on the settee. 'You said he was dead, and he's not.' All the energy had drained out of him.

'He wasn't a good dad. Or husband. He didn't tell the truth.' Isla could feel how hard it was for Mum to say this out loud.

Lac was quiet. He tugged and smoothed Luke Skywalker's tunic.

'He was a police spy,' Mum said.

Lac's eyes widened into deep pools. 'A SPY?' His spirit revived in an instant. 'Hear that, Luke? Dad was a spy. Awesome.'

'Not awesome,' Isla said. 'Awful. He was an undercover cop, spying on Mum and her friends.'

Archie whistled. 'Undercover? Cool. Like a secret agent.'

Lac jumped on the cushions and kneeled, facing Mum. 'Does 'undercover' mean in disguise?' He looked towards the closed door. 'I wonder what he'd look like with a long wig and glasses?'

Isla snorted. 'Jeez, Lac, it's not a dressing-up party.'

Mum said, 'Not disguise. Undercover means pretending to be someone you're not.' She sat down next to Lac. 'But it wasn't a game. He was paid to live a double life.'

Lac scratched his head, his eyes still wide with wonder.

'I can't explain it any better,' Mum said.

Isla bit her bottom lip. 'Wait a sec. Was he pretending to be our dad?'

Mum looked shocked. 'No! Of course not!' Worry lines carved diagonal grooves from her nose to the edges of her lips. 'That was the problem.'

'Problem?' Isla asked.

Mum stared ahead. Her lips were blubbery like uncooked sausages. She paused for a long time then spoke very quietly.

'The problem was, he loved you.'

'Me?' Isla's knees sagged. *Tick tick* filled the room.

Mum nodded.

'What about you?' Isla asked.

She spat out a throaty cackle. 'I don't know if he loved me or not. He said he did, but he's lied so much, how do I know if it's true?'

'What about me?' Lac piped up.

She squeezed him. 'You were our lovely baby.'

Mum's eyes were fixed on the curly patterns on the carpet. She shook her head, again and again. 'Not knowing, being taken in like that, treated like a fool, I'd been so stupid to believe it all – it was driving me mad.'

Archie cracked his knuckles and leant forward, knees widespread. 'This is incredible! What happened next?'

Isla wanted to knock his block off. 'Don't you dare laugh. This isn't a TV show, it's real life. It's our life. My messed up miserable life, so shut up will you.'

He shut up.

The branch made a *skrrrk* on the window. The cat stirred in its basket, stood up, turned round in a circle, lay down and curled up again. An eerie *who-ooh* groaned in the chimney.

'I was in deep trouble.' Isla jumped. Dad had appeared like a ghost. He stood in the open doorway. 'My bosses found out I had a wife. And children. I had to get away.'

CHAPTER 40

SORRY?

Grannie slid past Dad through the door, placed a plate of sandwiches on the table, and sank into her armchair by the fire.

'I heard that,' she said. 'How could you have kept it from me, your own mother?'

'The less you knew, the better. In case anyone came snooping, if you knew nothing, you couldn't answer any questions,' Dad said.

'Curious way to do your duty to your country.' Grannie's lips were set in a thin line.

The clock ticked. Isla walked over to the fireplace, picked up the little cross and stroked its patterns. She read the message engraved on its base: *Lachlan MacLean, Gus am bris an là.*

She forced herself to face Dad. 'Did your job matter more than your family? Did we never matter?'

Part of her realised she wasn't scared, and for once hiccups weren't threatening to ruin everything.

Still as a standing stone, Dad fixed his eyes on Luke Skywalker in Lac's hand. But Isla wouldn't leave him alone.

'When I was locked in an old couple's bathroom, I heard someone on the TV. Her husband was a police spy and he disappeared. Same as what happened to Mum.' She stopped for breath and placed her hands on her hips like Mrs Karim when she was telling someone off. 'What a coward, sneaking back to your parents.' Mrs Karim would have added: 'I'm disappointed in you.'

In the silence, Dad's mouth opened and closed. Leaning on the dresser, he tugged at his beard, as if that would make him speak. The lamb outside bleated again, and this time there was a gruff answering *baa*, which made it bleat even more.

'I –,' he said, then shook his head.

Tick tick. You're wasting time.

Isla was sizzling with fury. 'Say it. Say, "Yes, I lied."' Before he had time to answer, something clicked in her head. 'Hey, wait a minute. Did you lie about me too. Was I part of the job?'

'Like I said, I tried to keep you secret,' Dad said.

'Humph!' Isla said.

'Our little Isla,' Mum added.

'Isla what?'

A look passed between Mum and Dad.

'Isla McCluskey,' Mum said.

Isla's mouth dried up.

'You mean, I'm not Isla MacLean?'

'I changed your name to MacLean after he told me.'

'But not on my birth certificate? It wasn't lost, was it, when school asked for it? You just couldn't let me see it.'

Mum looked down at her grungy fingernails. She shook her head, her eyelids heavy with tears, hands hanging loosely from her knees. Lac put his arm round her, holding Luke in his other fist. 'If I had my lightsaber, I'd slash him,' he said, glaring at Dad. The cat washed its shoulder with a rasping tongue.

Isla's eyes glittered with rage. 'See what you did! Don't you care?'

He looked across the room at Mum. 'I'm so sorry.'

'Sorry? You treated Mum as a job, you disappeared, and you're *sorry?'* Once, on Coronation Street, a character had said "You're *sorry*?" in the same tone. Isla had thought it was stupid because how could you be *more* than sorry? But now she knew what it meant. 'Sorry isn't enough. You've got to –,' she threw her hands in the air, '– I don't know! Do something. Saying *sorry* doesn't make it okay that you abandoned us.'

'It wasn't like that,' he said in a husky voice. 'I loved you, our little family, but I was trapped. When they found out about you, I had to leave. For your own good.'

Mum winced.

'You deserted us,' Isla said.

Dad nodded towards Grannie. 'Ma and Da saved me, although they didn't know it.'

'Oh, we knew all right. But we had no idea what we'd saved you from. If we'd had an inkling, we'd have sent you straight back to your family.'

Dad hung his head, and Isla saw a bald patch she hadn't noticed before. 'I betrayed them, Ma. I was no good to them. No good to anyone.' A beam of sunshine from the window lit up tears glistening on his cheeks.

Isla could barely make out his mumbling words.

'It would have been better if you'd lost me at sea, not Da.'

That branch again. *Skrrrk.*

'You'd better leave now, son,' Grannie said. 'You've done enough damage for one day.' He left the room, the front door clicked, the gate crashed shut and a roar from the helicopter engine vibrated through the house.

Lac looked crestfallen. 'Flora said I could have another go in the 'copter.'

'Maybe tomorrow,' Grannie said. She spoke kindly to Mum. 'I hope you'll stay here for a wee while.'

Mum forced a weak smile. 'Thank you.'

Gusts of wind had blown away the rain clouds, and a momentary burst of sunshine flooded into the room. Grannie sat forward in her chair, prodded the fire with the poker and added another brick of peat.

'What a carry-on,' she muttered. As the flames flared, she warmed her hands, then turned back and opened her arms, knees spread wide. 'But as you're Sandy's children, then I'm surely your Grannie.'

It seemed like the whole world stopped. There was no sound from the wind outside, and the cat paused its fierce tongue-strokes, pink tongue sticking out of its mouth. *Tick, tick*. Lac threw Mum a questioning glance. She nodded. He rushed to the armchair and flung himself onto his new-found grannie.

Isla slumped in his place on the settee next to Mum. 'After hearing all that, I can't just say everything's okay.' Mum held her hand. 'I hate him. But he's gone, just like that. Is that it?'

'Are we ever going to see him again?' Lac asked, thumb in his mouth.

Isla's itches all flared up at once, and she wanted to scrape her skin until it was raw.

'I know it's a big shock, dear. It's a right mess and we're all upset. But I hope you're happy to find your Hebridean Grannie.'

'And cousin,' came across the room. Isla realised Archie had been quiet for ages. 'Sheesh, my Uncle Sandy's not who I thought.'

Isla frowned. 'I'm happy but not-happy at the same time.' Mum squeezed her hand.

'Of course, you are,' Grannie said. 'We'll sort it out, somehow. Now, how about a wee sandwich?'

Archie's long arm reached out and grabbed two sandwiches in one. Typical, thought Isla.

CHAPTER 41

MYSTERY UNRAVELLED

Mum knelt over Lac in the bath. Luke Skywalker dived into the water, and Mum laughed when he splashed her face and arms. 'Look Mum, he's jumped from a helicopter and saved an injured whale! He's a hero.'

'You two are heroes.' She sponged soapy water over his back.

'I'm gonna be a spy like Dad,' Lac said. Mum froze.

'Better not be,' Isla said.

Isla rubbed her head with a towel, wallowing in the ecstasy of Mum washing her hair in the bath. Their tiny squad, her and Lac, had travelled five hundred miles over land, across the sea, and through wild country to find Mum. They'd tramped almost the whole island, survived a storm, fed themselves (sort of), slept rough, got scared to death, drenched and boiled and stung, were captured and escaped again. Weasley had *died.*

And do you know what Mum said?

'Have you even washed since you left home?'

'MUMMEEE!!' they yelled.

And the second thing she said was, 'Don't get cocky. I'm back in charge now.'

Mummeee! Ally's favourite put-down sounded different. Isla understood something about Ally now she knew for herself how it felt to have no parents, even for a short time. Was *Mummeee* something Ally wished she could say, but she had no-one to say it to? Maybe Isla didn't hate her so much.

That woman on the TV had said she was in the dark for years, and when she found some answers, it was like reality turned on its head.

'We came to find you, and we sort of found ...'

'....Dadaidh,' Lac said. 'Will he come back tomorrow?'

'....and a Grannie and a cousin.'

'Mission accomplished,' Mum said.

Isla wondered. They were going home after the holidays, but it wouldn't be back to how it was. She wrapped the towel around her body and sat on the little stool, sliding her feet into a pair of woolly slippers. She rubbed her tummy, full of sausage and mash.

'Do you promise we'll come back and visit Dad? And Grannie?'

'And Archie,' added Lac.

'Promise.'

Lac stood up, and she wrapped a towel round him.

'And Flora – so I can learn to fly the helicopter.'

Things were starting to make sense. Isla realised why Mum had been sad for so long. She even understood why Mum had gone away. Just over a week ago, Isla was eating Weetabix and feeling lost. Now she was an agent who'd completed a successful mission, even though it hadn't turned out as she expected. The beginning of the journey, telling lies on the train and sneaking onto the ship, seemed such a long time ago. She didn't need to pretend anymore to people like the train guard, she could just be herself.

When she started this mission, she was just a kid. Now she was not 'just' anything anymore – just a girl, just a Year 7, just a deaf kid who writes poems and plays the trumpet, an oddball with a weird mum. *I'm me, an adventurer, traveller, explorer, survivor. A Brummie-Scot, MacLean, a girl with a new grannie and cousin.*

I'm a girl who has a dad.

The bathwater gurgled down the plughole.

'Mum,' she said over the noise, running her fingers through her clean hair.

'Mmm,' Mum said, her back to Isla.

'About Dad. Is he really all bad?' She tipped her head and fixed her zinger back in her ear. 'I'm trying to understand, but I don't get it. I mean, what if he wants to be our dad again?'

'I don't know, duck.' Mum handed her a small towel. 'Your hair's still dripping.'

'I know he's done bad things, and I hate him for that.' Isla squeezed drops of water out of her hair with the towel. 'But –' Isla didn't know how to say it, ' – inside, I might love him. A bit.'

Mum didn't look happy, but Isla was glad she said it.

'But I'll always love you more.'

'You don't need to say that,' Mum said.

Isla stroked her silky hair. 'It's true.'

As she watched Mum rubbing Lac with a towel, a flash of understanding sparked between them. They could see each other's soft spots, no more hiding or guessing.

Mum looked up. 'You've changed, Isla. You're not my babby anymore.'

Isla punched the air. 'At last!' She felt warm inside. 'Yeah, I do feel more.....me. I'll be thirteen next birthday. No-one is going to bully me from now on.'

Mum grinned, holding Lac in a tight hug, folded in the towel. 'Pass my specs, duck.'

'And Mum – ' Isla handed over her glasses. '– Lac sort of turned into a bird. He wouldn't talk, just squawked all the time.'

'Really?'

'Yes, really.'

'You've been so stressed and upset, I'm not surprised you're imagining things.'

'No Mum, it's true.'

'Come here, sweetie.' She opened the towel and pulled Isla into a three-way hug.

There are some things adults will never believe.

CHAPTER 42

HE CAN'T VANISH

Downstairs Isla flopped onto the settee, dry and warm, wearing one of Grannie's flowery nighties. Two cups of hot chocolate sat on the table with a plate of ginger biscuits. Isla dipped one in her mug. The cat was washing itself again, scraping its tongue over an extended back leg. Lac, drowned in a massive tee-shirt, stood with his arms folded around Grannie's middle, resting his head on her chest. 'I can hear your heart,' he said.

Grannie cleared her throat.

'Your dadaigh's coming to say goodnight.'

Isla's gulp of hot chocolate burned her throat.

'When?' she asked.

'Soon.'

Isla felt Mum stiffen next to her on the settee.

Grannie's kind voice said to her, 'It's the right thing, dearie. A man needs to see his children.'

Before Mum could reply, a car door banged outside. Moments later a rush of cold wind from the opening front door swept into the living room and a voice called,

'It's me, Ma.'

Mum stood up. 'I think I'll wait in the kitchen.'

Isla started to protest, but Grannie touched her arm to stop her.

A shape appeared in the doorway. Lac still had his arms around Grannie. Dad stepped into the room and ruffled Lac's hair. 'Hi Lachlan.'

Lac squirmed away. 'I'm Lac,' he said.

'Well, hello Lac,' Dad said. 'And hello to you too, Isla.'

Isla wished she wasn't wearing a silly nightie. She looked up at the red beard and pictured the crab tattoo under his shirt. 'Hello…' She paused, '…Dad.' It felt so weird saying that to a living man.

She looked over the top of her mug and waited for him to say something else. But she never expected what came out of his mouth next.

'Can we be friends?'

She started trembling all over. It was worse than hiccups. She forced herself to reply.

'I don't know… ' She tried to hold the cup still, and sipped the sugary hot chocolate. 'Not just like that, as if nothing has happened.' *Wow, where did that come from?* Isla stopped shaking.

It was Dad's turn to hesitate. 'I mean, can I get to know you so we can find out if we like each other?'

'Maybe.'

'And you too, little feller.'

'Maybe,' Lac parroted, 'if you give me loads of rides in the helicopter.'

Dad smiled, and looked back at Isla. 'I really want to.'

'Do you promise never to vanish again?'

'He can't!' Lac shouted. 'He's got to teach me how to be a pilot.'

'I promise.' The voice was serious, like Mrs Karim's but loads deeper.

Isla still didn't trust him. 'Grannie –' she liked that word a lot '– Grannie, how can we make sure he'll stick to his promise?'

Grannie pointed to the cross on the mantelpiece. 'Swear to your da's memory that you'll be true to your family.'

Dad picked up the cross. 'I swear, Da.'

Isla felt herself go hot. This was really happening. But one thing was stopping it from being totally amazing. She flicked her head towards Mum, who stood frozen with one hand on the kitchen doorknob.

Dad's eyes followed Isla's gesture. He took a step towards Mum, and with the same earnest tone, he spoke to her. 'I promise I'll never disappear again.'

Tick tick. Isla couldn't bear the silence. 'Mum! Answer him!'

In slow motion, Mum's frozen hand lifted off the doorknob and swept back her hair. 'Let's talk tomorrow,' she said.

Grannie sat on the arm of the settee and held out the ring to Mum. 'You should have this ring. It was my ma's, then mine. I gave it to Sandy for his wife.'

Mum recoiled. 'Mac wouldn't let me wear it. He said it was a secret ring.'

Grannie took Mum's hand and slipped the ring on her finger. 'Wear it. It means you belong with us.'

The silver shone as Mum's fingers turned the ring over and over just like Isla had done.

Grannie squinted at Isla. 'One day the ring will be yours.' Her face crinkled into a smile. 'From now on, my home is your home. And your dadaigh's, too.'

Isla held Mum's finger and ran her own fingertips up and round the interlocking shapes on the ring. 'What do these patterns mean, Grannie?' she asked.

'They mean eternal life. They go on forever. No beginning and no end. Like babies born into a family, new life carries on from the old.'

When Isla went to bed, she stood for a long time at the window. The sky looked like it was on fire, flames leaping between layers of cloud. Gradually, it subsided to an orange glow and Isla felt her whole self sucked into the huge pink light radiating across the horizon. As the dark rocks became black, the skyline faded to grey, and she could hardly tell the difference between sea and sky.

CHAPTER 43

A NEW FAMILY

A white-haired lady opened her front door and hung washing on her line to flap and dry in the strong wind. She paused to watch waves surging up the shore and a breeze tugging at the coats of two children running on the grass, chasing their Mum. The three of them crouched together on a grassy knoll, cocking their heads to one side, listening. *Swish-swoosh.* In-and-out, the surf crashed and receded. All three looked up at birds calling from the sky above: *Craark-craark, peeep, peep-peep, eeooooww-eeoww.*

Grannie opened her gate and waved.

'Mo chlann. My family,' she called.

'Halò, Granaidh!' Isla and Lac yelled back.

'Look over there!' She pointed to the sea in front of a rocky island. Isla saw a shiny black ball bobbing up and down with the waves, but it didn't move while the water washed around it.

'It's got eyes and whiskers like a cat!' Lac shouted, standing on tiptoes as if that would help him see better. 'It's looking straight at us!'

They watched the seal roll its eyes, blow air out through its nostrils and suck another load in, then sink down. The waters closed over its head, and it was gone.

'Seals are so beautiful,' Mum said.

'Don't be sad, Mum,' Lac said. 'It hasn't really disappeared.'

Isla's eyes were still glued to the spot where it had vanished. She knelt next to Mum. 'Isn't it strange to think that it's still there underwater. We didn't know it was there, but it's just that we can't see it.'

'There it is!' Lac shouted, pointing to a spot nearer the island. The seal's head looked even more like a ball, jogging in time to the sea's movements as if it belonged there. Which it did.

'That's like our family now,' Isla said, rolling onto her back. 'Even when we can't see it, we know it's there.'

Lac knelt beside them, still scanning the waves in case the seal returned. 'It's gonna come back,' he said.

'I mean,' Isla continued. 'Dad, Grannie, Archie – they were all here, but we didn't know.'

'Mmmm.' Sounded like Mum liked that idea.

'It's there now!' Lac shouted. 'And another one! And look, there's one slithering off the island into the water. There's millions of them. It's magic!'

Isla grinned. No need for Hermione anymore. They'd made their own magic.

– THE END –

Acknowledgements

I've discovered that it takes a horde of supporters to create a book. Huge thanks to Rose Drew and Alan Gillott at Stairwell Books for believing in Isla and Lac's story, and to Dawn Treacher for the superb illustrations.

I am eternally grateful to readers whose detailed critical feedback of various drafts helped to shape the story: Clare Weze, Curtis Chin, Heather Leach, Sue Browning, Steve Smythe, Honor Somerset, Anna Fleur Rawlinson and Sheryl Crown. I was spurred on by the enthusiasm and ideas from Miss Ogden's Year 6 class at Greenbank Primary school. Further thanks to the online group at the Society of Children's Book Writers and Illustrators (SCBWI) for help in making each chapter a page-turner for young readers.

Lily Rose Hamilton was the first child to read the full manuscript of *Mission: Find Mum*. She read the whole book out loud to her mother, and her endorsement means the world to me.

Thanks to Sarah Wimperis' Year 6 book group at Westwood Academy for their enthusiastic reading and discussion. And thanks to Deborah Cox for gathering opinion from teachers about certain points in the plot.

I'm indebted to Clare Weze, Jennifer Burkinshaw and Jane Houng for providing their reactions to the final manuscript.

I wouldn't have got here without my Artists' Way buddy Lorna Tittle, and the support and guidance from teaching staff on the University of Salford's Creative Writing: Innovation and Experiment MA course. Thank you all.

And above all, thanks to Liz Clarke, my wife and fellow-adventurer in the Hebridean islands where the story of Isla and Lac's mission sparked into life.

Resources

A note for children about wellbeing

If you feel affected by any of the issues in this book and would like to talk to someone, contact Childline online www.childline.co.uk or by phone 0800 1111. Childline can help you with things like family problems, bullying, feeling different, living with disability, and coping with anxiety.

Everyone deserves to feel generally positive about their life. Talking to another person can make a huge difference.

Other books for young people available from Stairwell Books

100 Summers	Ali Sparkes
The Broke Hotel	Clayton Lister
A Mouse's Tail	Red Tower
My Sister is a Dog	Ali Sparkes
Ivy Elf's Magical Mission	Elisabeth Kelly
Pandemonium of Parrots	Dawn Treacher
The Pirate Queen	Charlie Hill
Harriet the Elephotamus	Fiona Kirkman
A Business of Ferrets	Alwyn Bathan
Shadow Cat Summer	Rebecca Smith
Very Bad Gnus	Suzanne Sheran
The Water Bailiff's Daughter	Yvonne Hendrie
Season of the Mammoth	Antony Wootten
The Grubby Feather Gang	Antony Wootten
Mouse Pirate	Dawn Treacher
Rosie and John's Magical Adventure	The Children of Ryedale District Primary Schools

For further information please contact rose@stairwellbooks.com

www.stairwellbooks.co.uk
@stairwellbooks

Milton Keynes UK
Ingram Content Group UK Ltd.
UKHW030801130824
446857UK00001B/7

9 781913 432942